PENGUIN ARCHIVE

Monkey King Makes Havoc in Heaven

Wu Cheng'en

c. 1506–1582

A PENGUIN SINCE 1961

Wu Cheng'en
Monkey King Makes Havoc in Heaven

Translated by Julia Lovell

PENGUIN ARCHIVE

PENGUIN BOOKS

UK | USA | Canada | Ireland | Australia
India | New Zealand | South Africa

Penguin Books is part of the Penguin Random House group of companies whose addresses can be found at global.penguinrandomhouse.com.

Penguin Random House UK,
One Embassy Gardens, 8 Viaduct Gardens, London SW11 7BW

penguin.co.uk

The translation of *Monkey King* first published in Penguin Classics 2021
This extract published in Penguin Classics 2025
001

Translation copyright © Julia Lovell, 2021

No part of this book may be used or reproduced in any manner for the purpose of training artificial intelligence technologies or systems. In accordance with Article 4(3) of the DSM Directive 2019/790, Penguin Random House expressly reserves this work from the text and data mining exception.

Set in 12/15pt Dante MT Std
Typeset by Jouve (UK), Milton Keynes
Printed and bound in Great Britain by Clays Ltd, Elcograf S.p.A.

The authorized representative in the EEA is Penguin Random House Ireland, Morrison Chambers, 32 Nassau Street, Dublin D02 YH68

A CIP catalogue record for this book is available from the British Library

ISBN: 978-0-241-75240-1

Penguin Random House is committed to a sustainable future
for our business, our readers and our planet. This book is made from
Forest Stewardship Council® certified paper.

Chapter One

After Pan Gu created the universe, by separating earth and sky with his mighty ax, the world was divided into four continents, in the north, south, east, and west. Our story takes place in the east.

By a great ocean lay a land called Aolai, within which was a mountain called Flower-Fruit, home to sundry immortals. What a mountain it was: of crimson ridges and strange boulders, phoenixes and unicorns, evergreen grasses and immortal peaches. And on its peak sat a divine stone, thirty-six and a half feet high, twenty-four in circumference.

Since creation, this rock had been nourished by heaven and earth, the sun and the moon, until it was divinely inspired with an immortal embryo, and one day gave birth to a stone egg, about as large as a ball. After exposure to the air, it turned into a stone monkey, with perfectly sculpted features and limbs. This monkey learned to climb and run, then bowed in all four directions of the compass. Two golden rays shone from his eyes all the way to the Palace of the Polestar, startling the benevolent sage of Heaven, the Jade Emperor, while he sat on his throne in the Hall of Divine Mists surrounded by his immortal ministers. The emperor ordered two of his generals, Thousand-Mile Eye and Follow-the-Wind Ear, to look out of the South Gate of Heaven and locate the source of this light. 'Your humble servants,' they soon reported back, 'have traced it back to Flower-Fruit Mountain, in the small country of Aolai on the eastern continent, where a rock has given birth to an egg, which has turned into a stone monkey, whose golden eyes have dazzled even Your Majesty. But now the monkey has paused for some refreshment, and the blaze has dimmed.'

'The creatures of the mortal world are all born from heaven and earth,' the Jade Emperor remarked tolerantly. 'Nothing they do can surprise us.'

The monkey gamboled over the mountains, eating grass, drinking from streams, picking mountain flowers, hunting for fruit; he kept company with wolves and snakes, tigers and panthers, befriended deer and antelope, and swore brotherhood with macaques and apes. At night, he slept below cliffs; at sunrise, he wandered through mountains and caves, with no sense of the passing of time.

One sweltering morning, he sheltered from the

heat with a crowd of monkeys in the shade of some pines; they swung from branch to branch, built sand pagodas, and chased dragonflies and lizards. Afterward, bathing in a mountain stream, they noticed how its current seemed to tumble like rolling melons and wondered where it was coming from. 'As we don't have anything particular to do today,' one of them suggested, 'let's follow the stream to its origin.' With shrieks of happy agreement, they all scrambled up the mountain to a great curtain of a waterfall.

The monkeys clapped their hands in delight. 'Whoever dares pass through the waterfall to discover the source of the water, and returns alive, can be our king.'

After three calls for a volunteer, the stone monkey suddenly jumped out of the crowd. 'I'll go!' This excellent monkey closed his eyes, crouched, then sprang with one bound through the sheet of water. Once on the other side, he opened his eyes. Before him was a gleaming iron bridge, under which flowed the source of the stream. From the bridge, he could see into a beautiful cave residence: cushioned with moss, hung with stalactites, furnished with carved benches and beds, and equipped with pans and stoves. In the middle of the bridge hung a stone tablet on which was written, in large, regular calligraphy, the following address:

Wu Cheng'en

HEAVENLY WATER-CURTAIN CAVE THE BLESSED LAND OF FLOWER-FRUIT MOUNTAIN

The stone monkey leaped back out through the waterfall. 'Fantastic luck!' he whooped.

'What's it like inside?' the other monkeys crowded around to ask. 'How deep is the water?'

'It's the perfect place for us to make our home, an ideal refuge from Heaven's fits of temper,' explained the stone monkey, and described the wonders of Water-Curtain Cave. 'It could easily hold thousands of us. Let's move in straightaway.'

'You go first and we'll follow behind!' yelped the others.

Once more, the stone monkey crouched, shut his eyes, and sprang through the water. 'Come on!' he called. The braver of the monkeys immediately followed; the more nervous ones tweaked their ears, scratched their cheeks, stretched, and chattered a good deal before eventually leaping onto the bridge and into the cave. Once there, they were soon snatching at bowls, fighting over stoves and beds, and dragging things back and forth – for such is the mischief of monkeys. There was not a moment's peace until they'd fretted themselves into exhaustion.

The stone monkey spoke again: 'A monkey stands

and falls by his word.* You promised that whoever dared pass through the waterfall and returned safely would be king. So what are you waiting for?'

Without a murmur of dissent, the monkeys immediately bowed and wished their new king a long, long life. Their new ruler quickly dropped his old name – Stone Monkey – in favor of Beautiful Monkey King and appointed a few of the monkeys to ministerial and civil service positions. The monkeys then devoted themselves to exploring the delights of Flower-Fruit Mountain by day and returning to Water-Curtain Cave at night.

The Beautiful Monkey King lived this happy, innocent life for somewhere between three and four hundred years. Then one day, while banqueting with the other monkeys, he suddenly became melancholy and began to weep. 'What has upset our great king?' clamored the others.

'I fear for the future,' the monkey king explained with a sigh.

'But we live in bliss,' said his subjects, laughing, 'slaves of neither the unicorn, the phoenix, nor man. Why are you worrying about the future?'

'Life is good now,' the monkey king said, 'but

* The original Chinese is a quotation from Confucius, *The Analects*.

eventually we will grow old and fall into the clutches of Yama, King of the Underworld.'

While the monkey masses – instantly fearful – buried their faces in their hands and mewled piteously, a long-armed ape jumped out of the crowd: 'Our great king's new sense of mortality suggests the beginnings of a religious calling. Only three types of creature can escape King Yama and his wheel of life and death: Buddhas, immortals, and holy sages.'

'Where are they to be found?' asked the monkey king.

'In ancient caves on divine mountains.'

'I leave immediately,' declared the monkey king. 'Even if my quest takes me to the very end of the world, I will return with the secret of eternal life.'

All the monkeys applauded wildly. 'Marvelous! First, though, we will gather fruits from far away for a huge send-off feast.' The next day was taken up with preparing and consuming this banquet, an extraordinary spread of plums, cherries, lychees, pears, dates, peaches, strawberries, almonds, walnuts, chestnuts, hazelnuts, tangerines, sugarcane, persimmons and pomegranates, and coconut and grape wine. The monkey king sat at the head of the tables, with his subjects approaching in turn, in strict order of age and rank, to toast him with wine, flowers, and fruit.

The following day, the monkey king rose early.

'Make me a dry pinewood raft, little monkeys, and fetch me a bamboo pole and some fruit for the journey.' When all was ready, he hopped onto the raft and, pushing off with all his might, set off across the ocean. He was in luck, for a strong southeasterly wind blew him directly to the northwest coast of the southern continent. When his bamboo pole told him he was in shallow water, he abandoned the raft for the shoreline, where he encountered humans hunting for fish, wild geese, and clams and dredging salt.

He ran at them, making strange faces, and they dropped their baskets and nets and scattered in terror. The monkey king grabbed the slowest of them and stripped him of his clothes. After dressing in them, Monkey made a tour of the continent's towns and cities, studying human manners and speech. Eight or nine years passed. Monkey remained determined to seek the formula for eternal life, while the humans who surrounded him sought only money and fame, without a thought for their own mortality; no one cared what became of him.

Eventually, Monkey came to the Western Ocean. Still in search of immortals, he built himself another raft and floated across to the western continent. In time, he approached a beautiful, jagged mountain, thickly forested at its base and luxuriant with flowers, grasses, mosses, bamboo, and pines – an ideal hermit's refuge. Unconcerned about the danger of wolves, snakes, tigers, or leopards, Monkey climbed up to look around. When he reached the top, he suddenly heard a human voice singing deep within a copse of trees.

> I sleep till dawn then wander the wood,
> cutting creepers for my livelihood.
> When I've gathered as much as I can hold,
> I stroll singing through the market till it's sold.
> I trade my load for wine and rice,
> and never haggle over the price.
> Living without ambition or conceit,
> only immortals and Taoists will I meet.

'At last!' the monkey king rejoiced to himself. Skipping through the forest, he came face-to-face with a woodcutter busy at work, dressed in a large conical hat made of young bamboo, a cotton-gauze tunic with a silk sash, and straw sandals. 'Salutations, immortal!' Monkey hailed him.

The flustered woodcutter dropped his ax. 'Hush! I am a poor, ignorant man unable even to feed or clothe myself.'

'Why, then, do you sing about immortals?' Monkey asked him.

The woodcutter laughed: 'Oh, that. A neighbor of mine, an immortal as it happens, taught the song to

Monkey King Makes Havoc in Heaven

me, to cheer me up when life was getting me down. A moment ago, I started worrying about something, so I sang it. I didn't know anyone was listening.'

'Why don't you become his disciple? You could learn the secret of eternal life.'

'I've not had an easy life,' the woodcutter explained. 'My father died when I was seven or eight. I'm an only child, and have been my mother's sole support ever since. And now that she's getting old, she needs me all the more. All we have is the rice and tea I get in exchange for my firewood. I can't abandon her for a religious life.'

'Well, I'm sure you will be rewarded in later life for your filial devotion. In the meantime, though, could you point the way to the immortal's house, so that I can pay him a visit?'

'It's not far. This is Heart and Soul Mountain. About seven or eight miles to the south, you'll come to the Cave of the Tilted Moon and Three Stars, the home of an immortal called Subodhi, who has trained many disciples, and currently has thirty or forty studying under him.'

Monkey tugged at the woodcutter. 'Come with me! You won't regret it.'

'Did you not listen to anything I said just now?' he answered, exasperated. 'I've wood to chop. On your way now.'

So Monkey left the woodcutter and found the path to the south. After seven or eight miles, a heavenly cave dwelling came into sight, shrouded in mists and light, framed by an emerald-green forest of bamboo and cypress and by moss-covered hanging cliffs. Cranes, phoenixes, apes, deer, lions, and elephants roamed about. The entrance was tightly sealed and the place seemed uninhabited, but a huge stone slab – thirty feet tall by eight feet wide – told Monkey that the woodcutter had spoken the truth: THE CAVE OF THE TILTED MOON AND THREE STARS, HEART AND SOUL MOUNTAIN. Not daring to knock, Monkey loitered on a nearby pine, nibbling some nuts.

After a very short while, the door creaked open and a young immortal of exceptionally refined looks emerged. He wore a robe with loose, billowing sleeves; his hair was bound with silk cords. 'Who's making all that noise?'

Jumping down from the tree, Monkey bowed. 'I didn't mean to disturb you. I'm here to learn the secret of eternal life.'

'You seek the Way, you say?' The young man smiled. 'Our master just told me to look outside the front door for a new student.'

'That would be me!' exclaimed Monkey.

'Come on, then,' the young man said, ushering him inside.

Monkey King Makes Havoc in Heaven

Monkey followed the youth deep into the cave, past story upon story and row upon row of jeweled pavilions, towers, and arches, until they reached the foot of a jade platform, on top of which sat Subodhi, the famous Patriarch of the West; thirty trainee immortals sat on the ground below. 'Master!' Monkey gasped, launching into a frenzy of kowtows.

'Tell me your name and where you're from,' Subodhi asked, 'before you smash your head beyond repair.'

'I come from Water-Curtain Cave on Flower-Fruit Mountain in the land of Aolai on the eastern continent.'

'Throw him out!' Subodhi roared. 'Liars can't learn enlightenment! Two oceans and the southern continent lie between here and Aolai.'

Monkey resumed his kowtowing, this time at double speed. 'It's true!' he protested. 'My journey here took more than ten years.'

'Hmpf,' conceded Subodhi. 'That sounds about right. So what's your name? Who were your parents?'

'I have no parents,' Monkey replied.

'Were you born from a tree, then?'

'All I can remember is an immortal rock on Flower-Fruit Mountain. One year, it split open, and there I was.'

'I see,' considered Subodhi, hiding his delight at

this revelation. 'So you were born of heaven and earth. Get up and walk about, so I can look at you.' Monkey scampered this way and that. 'You're not exactly classically handsome,' Subodhi said, laughing, 'but you look exactly as a monkey reared on fruit and nuts ought to. I'll give you a surname: Sun. Written one way, it means monkey. But I'll drop the animal radical, leaving us with the *Sun* that means child.'

Monkey burbled with glee. 'A surname! I've got a surname! But can I have a given name also, so that you can easily call me hither and thither?'

'The given names of my disciples rotate within a cycle of twelve characters.'

'And those twelve characters are?'

'Broad, *guang*; great, *da*; wise, *zhi*; intelligent, *hui*; true, *zhen*; obedient, *ru*; of nature, *xing*; of the sea, *hai*; outstanding, *ying*; awoken, *wu*; rounded, *yuan*; enlightened, *jue*. As you fall into the tenth, "awoken," *wu*, I will call you Sun Wukong: Sun-who-has-awoken-to-emptiness. Happy with that?'

'Sun Wukong!' Monkey chortled. 'I love it!'

The name spoke an important truth: for at the beginning of everything, there were no names – only emptiness. To advance from emptiness, living creatures must first become aware of it.

And if you wish to know what Monkey learned next, you must read on.

Chapter Two

While Monkey pranced delightedly about, Subodhi ordered the congregation to take him away and teach him some basic rules of hygiene and etiquette. The disciples found Monkey a place in the corridor where he could sleep, and the following morning he began to learn from his fellow students how to speak and behave. Day in, day out, they discussed scriptures and doctrines; he practiced calligraphy and burned incense. In his spare time, he swept the ground and weeded the gardens, tended to the trees and flowers, gathered wood and lit fires, and fetched water and carried drinks. Six or seven perfectly contented years slipped by. Eventually, Subodhi climbed back onto his rostrum and summoned his immortals for a lecture on doctrine: a synthesis of Taoism, Buddhism, and Confucianism.

In the audience, Wukong began fidgeting, even dancing, with enthusiasm. Subodhi singled him out for a scolding: 'Why can't you stand still and listen?'

'Forgive me! I was too excited by what you were saying.'

'Seeing as you're clever enough to understand my lecture, can you tell me how long you've lived in our cave?'

'I fear I've completely lost track of time,' Monkey replied. 'All I know is that the peach trees on the mountain have fruited seven times.'

'If you've eaten your way through seven peach seasons, you must have been here for seven years. What is it that you want to learn from me?'

'A little Taoism would do nicely, Master.'

'There are three hundred and sixty subcategories of Taoism; each can lead to enlightenment. Which do you wish to study?'

'Whichever you think best,' Monkey answered.

'How about the division of Art?' suggested Subodhi.

'What would that involve?'

'Summoning immortals, divining with yarrow stalks, and learning to pursue good and shun evil.'

'Will it make me live forever?' Monkey wanted to know.

'Not a chance,' Subodhi replied.

'Then I'll have nothing to do with it,' Monkey responded.

'How about the division of the Schools, then?

That would cover the Confucians, the Buddhists, the Taoists, the Yin-and-Yangists, the Mohists, and the Physicians. It's mainly reading scriptures and chanting prayers.'

'Is this the road to immortality?'

'If it's immortality you seek, this division is about as useful as building a pillar in a wall.'

'I'm not fluent in your Taoist argot. What do you mean by that?'

'If you want a house to last, you gird the walls with pillars. All the same, one day the house will fall into ruin; such is the way of the material world.'

'Then I'll have nothing to do with the Schools, either.'

'How about the division of Silence?' the Patriarch now suggested. 'You learn fasting and abstinence, quietism and inaction, meditating cross-legged, vows of silence and vegetarianism, yoga and solitary retreats.'

'But will it make me immortal?'

'It will make you no stronger than an unfired brick on the kiln.'

'Another circumlocution! Now what do you mean?'

'An unfired brick may look like a brick, but it has not yet been hardened by fire and water. It will disintegrate at the first heavy rainfall.'

'Not for me, then!'

'Can I interest you in Action? This one will keep you busy. You have to gather the yin to nourish the yang, bend the bow and tread the arrow, rub the navel to induce the qi. There's also a certain amount of alchemical experimentation involved: burning rushes, forging cauldrons, swallowing red lead, and drinking virgins' menstrual blood, boys' urine, and married women's breast milk. That kind of thing.'

'Surely that will bring immortality?'

'To gain immortality from such a method is as easy as fishing the moon out of the water.'

'Not again! Speak plainly.'

'When the moon is high, it leaves a reflection in the water, but you can't actually fish it out, for it is only an illusion.'

'No thanks!' Monkey snorted.

The exasperated Subodhi now jumped off his rostrum. 'You monkey, you!' he shouted. 'Nothing's good enough!' He hit Monkey three times on the head with a ruler, then walked back to his room, hands behind his back, and shut the door, ignoring the rest of his horrified audience.

'Where are your manners?' the other disciples berated Monkey. 'Master Subodhi offered you all sorts of doctrines; why did you reply so rudely? Now you've gone and offended him. Who knows when he'll come out again?'

Unfazed, Monkey smiled from ear to ear, for he had instantly understood Subodhi's hidden meaning. By hitting him three times, his teacher was surely telling him to visit at the third watch – around midnight. By folding his hands behind his back and shutting the main doors, he was instructing Monkey to come by the back entrance so that he could be taught in secret.

Monkey was irrepressibly cheerful all day, whiling away the hours with his fellow students at the entrance to the cave, impatiently awaiting nightfall. At dusk, he lay down to sleep with the others, pretended to close his eyes, and steadied his breathing. Since there was no watchman in the mountains to beat the hour, Monkey could only guess the time from the number of breaths he had taken. When he estimated that the appointed hour had come, he quietly got up, dressed, opened the door, and stole away from the crowd of sleeping disciples.

Guided by a clear moon and the darting glow of fireflies, he made his way to the back door into Subodhi's room, which he discovered was open. 'So I was right!' he congratulated himself. He slipped in and knelt by Subodhi's bed, where the master was curled up asleep, facing the wall. Soon, Subodhi awoke, stretched his legs, and murmured a poem:

> The Way is mysterious,
> and the golden elixir rare.
> If you reveal magic to an imperfect being
> your words will be empty and your tongue dry!

Monkey took this as his cue to speak: 'I'm waiting.'

Subodhi pulled on his clothes, then sat back down cross-legged. 'Monkey! What are you doing here?'

'You told me to come through the back door at the third watch, for a lesson in enlightenment.'

'This chap truly is a child of heaven and earth,' Subodhi rejoiced to himself. 'How else could he have unriddled me so easily?'

'I have come alone,' Monkey went on, 'in the hope that Master will teach me the Way of Immortality.'

'This is your destiny,' Subodhi replied. 'Come close and listen.'

Monkey kowtowed his thanks, washed his ears out, and kneeled to hear Subodhi's secret life-preserving precepts.

Thus Monkey was blessed with understanding. After memorizing the magic formula and kowtowing fulsome thanks to Subodhi, he returned quietly to his own bed as the sun rose. The moment he sat down, he shook off his coverlet. 'It's morning! Time to get up!' His fellow students had slept through all that had happened to Monkey during the night. As the weeks and months went by, he outwardly played the class fool, while secretly practicing what he had learned in noontime breathing exercises.

Another three years passed before Subodhi reappeared to teach his disciples. He spoke of academic debates and parables and of external self-cultivation. 'Where's Monkey?' he suddenly asked.

Monkey kneeled before him. 'Here I am!'

'What have you been working on of late?'

'The basics of immortality: the nature and origins of all things.'

'In that case, you have already penetrated the divine substance of matter. But beware of the peril of the three calamities.'

Monkey mulled this over for a while. 'Master is surely mistaken,' he eventually responded. 'I thought that anyone who has learned the Way and is rich in virtue will live as long as Heaven itself. Neither fire, nor water, nor illness can harm him. What three calamities do you speak of?'

'What you have learned is not ordinary magic. You have stolen the creative power of heaven and earth itself, and penetrated the dark formulae of the sun and the moon. Ghosts and spirits will seek to bring you down. Although you have extended your life, in five hundred years' time Heaven will unleash the calamity of thunder at you. You must seek wisdom to prevent this peril. Succeed and you will live as long as Heaven itself. Fail and you will die. In another five hundred years, Heaven will rain the calamity of the cold, dark fire of yin. It burns from the soles of your feet to the cavity of your heart. It will reduce your entrails to ashes and your limbs to ruins. Your millennium of hard work will then be as dust and nothingness. After another five hundred years, Heaven will set the calamity of wind onto you. This is no earthly wind. It enters through the fontanels, blows through the six internal organs, midriff, and nine orifices. Your flesh and bones will dissolve and your body will disintegrate. You see, then, why I recommend avoiding these calamities.'

Monkey's fur stood on end. 'Tell me how to escape these horrors!'

'Normally, this would be perfectly simple. But as you are an unusual specimen, I fear I cannot teach you.'

'I've a head at the top and feet at the bottom, nine apertures, four limbs, five viscera, and six internal organs. How am I unusual?'

'You bear a superficial resemblance to humans, but your cheeks are abnormally flat.' (Monkeys have rather angular faces, with sunken cheeks and pointed muzzles.)

Monkey patted his face combatively. 'Appearances can be deceptive. My cheek pouches have storage capacity on the inside. I demand parity.'

'Fair enough,' considered Subodhi. 'Which escape do you want to learn? There's the Art of the Big Dipper, which involves thirty-six transformations, or the Art of the Earthly Multitude, which involves seventy-two.'

'The more the merrier,' considered Monkey. 'I'll take the second.'

'Come over here, then, and I will tell you the formula.'

No one knows what Subodhi whispered into Monkey's ear. But our hero was someone who could learn a hundred things from a single explanation. He immediately memorized the magic and, after practicing on his own, mastered the seventy-two transformations.

One day, as the community was enjoying the scenery at dusk in front of the Cave of the Tilted Moon and Three Stars, Subodhi suddenly turned to Monkey. 'How are you getting on?'

'Thanks to you, I am now fully perfected. I can float and fly, as light as mist.'

'Let's see you do it.'

Anxious to show off, Monkey somersaulted some sixty feet into the air. In the time it would take to eat a meal, he had covered three miles. He returned and stood before Subodhi. 'I call this cloud-galloping.'

Subodhi snorted. 'Cloud-crawling, more like. Any self-respecting immortal can fit in a tour of the four oceans between breakfast and dinner. *That's* cloud-galloping. In fact, given that it took you most of the day to travel just three miles, cloud-crawling is an overstatement.'

'What you describe is fiendishly hard!'

'Nothing in this world is hard. It is only the mind that makes it so.'

'If you're going to help me, then do it properly. Please teach me how to cloud-gallop.'

'Immortals begin a cloud-gallop by stamping their feet,' Subodhi explained. 'But when you took off just now, you jumped. So I'll give you a lift-off that suits you: the cloud-somersault.'

Subodhi taught him a magic sign and spell. 'Now clench your fists, shake your body, and jump. A single somersault will carry you 108,000 miles.'

'Lucky Monkey!' The crowd of disciples giggled. 'If you master this, you can get a job as an express courier. You'll always be able to make a living.'

As dusk was now turning to darkness, master and disciples went back inside the cave. But Monkey stayed up all night until he had mastered the cloud-somersault. Day in, day out, he reveled in the freedom of his new immortality.

One day, as spring was giving way to summer, Subodhi's disciples gathered under a pine tree to chat. 'You must have some extraordinary karma stored up from a previous existence,' the others said to Monkey. 'The other day, Master whispered instructions to you for avoiding the three calamities. Have you got the hang of them?'

'Thanks to Subodhi's teaching and practicing hard,' Monkey said, smiling, 'I know what I'm doing.'

'Show and tell, then.'

Monkey decided to make an exhibition of himself. 'What do you want me to turn into?'

'How about a pine tree?' Monkey made the magic sign, recited the spell, and became a pine tree: tall, straight, and elegant, without the slightest simian semblance. The disciples laughed and clapped. 'Marvelous monkey!'

The hullabaloo roused Subodhi, who hurried out with his staff. 'Who's making all this racket?'

The disciples immediately hushed themselves while Monkey resumed his original form. 'We were just chatting, Master.'

'You should be ashamed of yourselves!' roared Subodhi. 'Those seeking the Way should not open their mouths so freely, for fear of scattering their vital forces or causing arguments through loose talk. What were you shouting and laughing about, anyway?'

'Monkey was entertaining us with a transformation,' the disciples confessed. 'We asked him to turn into a pine tree and our cheering disturbed you, Master. Please forgive us.'

'Go away, all of you. Except you, Sun Wukong: come here!' Once the others had scattered, a proper scolding began. 'What do you think you're doing, turning into a pine tree? Why did you show them what you can do? If you saw someone with exceptional powers, wouldn't you want them, too? Sooner or later, your fellow disciples will ask you for the magic. If you're weak enough not to refuse them, you'll spill the secret. If you don't tell them, they might force it out of you. You are no longer safe here.'

'Please forgive me!' begged Monkey, kowtowing.

'No hard feelings. But you must leave.'

Monkey's eyes filled with tears. 'Where are you sending me?'

'You must go back to where you came from. You won't last long here.'

Monkey was overcome with regret. 'I have been away from home for twenty years. Though I yearn to see my former subjects again, I hate to leave you before I have repaid your kindness to me.'

'Forget it,' said the Patriarch. 'Just don't drag me into any of your messes.'

Seeing that there was no point in arguing, Monkey took respectful leave of Subodhi and his fellow disciples.

Before he left, Subodhi remade his earlier point more forcefully. 'After you leave this place, you're bound to get up to no good. I don't care what villainy you perpetrate; just don't tell anyone that you were my disciple. If you breathe a word of what I did for you, I'll flay your wretched monkey carcass, grind your bones to dust, and banish your soul permanently to the Place of Ninefold Darkness. And I'll only be getting started.'

'Right you are. If anyone asks, I'll tell them I'm self-taught.' Monkey launched into a cloud-somersault eastward. Soon enough, he landed back on Flower-Fruit Mountain, rejoicing at how easy his return was, compared with his arduous outward journey.

Just as he was trying to work out which path to take back to Water-Curtain Cave, he heard the cries of cranes and monkeys echoing about him. 'I'm back, little ones!' he called.

From out of rocky enclaves, grasses, flowers, and

trees, thousands of monkeys of different sizes leaped out and surrounded their king. 'Why were you gone so long? A cruel demon has attacked Water-Curtain Cave, stolen our possessions, and kidnapped our children.'

'Who is this insolent fiend?' raged Monkey. 'Tell me everything, and I'll settle his hash.'

'He calls himself the Monstrous King of Chaos, and he lives north of here.'

'How far?'

'We don't know. He arrives like the clouds and departs like the mist, wind, rain, thunder, and lightning.'

'Very well. Amuse yourselves while I go and find him.'

Monkey cloud-somersaulted northward, landing on top of a rugged, precipitous mountain. As he surveyed the area, he heard voices. Coming down to investigate, he discovered a number of imps dancing about in front of a cliffside establishment named Watery-Innard Cave. They fled as soon as Monkey appeared. 'Stay where you are!' he commanded. 'I've a message for you to pass on. I am the King of Water-Curtain Cave on Flower-Fruit Mountain, due south of here. Because this Havoc Monster, or what have you, of yours has repeatedly terrorized my people, I've come to settle the score.'

Monkey King Makes Havoc in Heaven

The imps rushed into the cave. 'O great king!' they wailed. 'Catastrophe!'

'What are you talking about?' the Monstrous King – for it was he – asked. After the fiends reported their encounter outside the cave, their sovereign laughed: 'Those monkeys are always saying they have a king who left them to study the Way. So he's back at last, it seems. How is he dressed, and what weapons does he have?'

'None that we can see. He's bareheaded and is wearing a red robe tied with a yellow sash and black boots. He doesn't resemble your regular Buddhist or Taoist. But he's certainly making quite a racket out there.'

'Bring me my armor and my weapon,' instructed the monster. Once dressed for combat, he exited the cave with his retinue of goblins. 'So where's this King of Water-Curtain Cave?' he bellowed.

Monkey gazed upon a demon thirty feet high, with a waist as thick as ten arm-spans and brandishing a sharp, bright sword. He wore a black silk robe, a black iron breastplate pulled tight with leather straps, and ornately decorated boots; his black helmet glinted in the sunlight. This, in sum, was the Monster of Havoc, and he did not look like a pushover.

'Behold Monkey!' Monkey introduced himself.

Finally locating Monkey on the ground beneath him, the monster laughed. 'You're less than four feet tall and unarmed. How dare you challenge me?'

'Reckless fiend!' Monkey yelled back. 'Think I look small? I can grow in the blink of an eye. And as for a weapon: I can hook the moon down from the sky. Eat my fist!' He sprang up and began showering the monster's face with blows.

The monster blocked them with one hand. 'Look, gnome, I'd be a laughingstock if I were to kill you with my sword. I'll lay down my weapon and we can have a boxing match instead.'

'Gladly!' cheered Monkey, and the two set to hammering each other. In this kind of combat, long arms sometimes throw inaccurate punches; short-range strikes can be more precise. Monkey pummeled his opponent's ribs and made a direct hit in the crotch. Knocked off balance, his opponent picked up his huge steel sword again and hacked away at Monkey, who smartly stepped back and out of range.

Realizing that the fight was getting serious, Monkey deployed the Body Beyond the Body Magic: he plucked a handful of hairs, chewed them to pieces, then spat them out, shouting 'Change!' The hairs transformed into two or three hundred little monkeys, who crowded around their adversary. When someone becomes an immortal, you see, he can transform his spirit at will. Now that Monkey was an adept in the Way, every single one of the eighty-four thousand hairs on his body could change into whatever form he wanted. His mini-monkeys were so sharp-eyed and agile that the monster couldn't get his sword near them. Back and forth they weaved and darted until the monster was completely surrounded. Some squeezed, some tugged, some jabbed at his crotch, while others pulled at his feet, tore his hair, gouged at his eyes, tweaked his nose, and generally befuddled him. While this was going on, the real Monkey managed to grab the monster's sword, advance through the mass of little monkeys, and slice the monster's head in two. Monkey then led his army into the cave, where they slaughtered all the imps. The conquest complete, Monkey shook himself and the hairs returned to his body.

About forty monkeys, however, retained their shape – for they had been kidnapped here from Flower-Fruit Mountain – and tearfully explained themselves to the monkey king. 'These stone pots and bowls' – they gestured around the cave – 'he also stole from us.'

'Then we will take them with us,' pronounced Monkey, who then set fire to the cave and burned it to ashes. 'Let's head home,' he told his followers. 'Close your eyes and don't be afraid.'

That marvelous monkey muttered a spell, swept up the others in a wind-propelled cloud, and landed smoothly back on Flower-Fruit Mountain. 'Open your eyes, little ones.' Immediately recognizing their old home, the delighted monkeys rushed into the cave and lined up with the others before Monkey. They held a celebratory banquet of fruits and wine, during which Monkey regaled them with the story of how he had defeated the monster.

'Where were you all that time, great king?' they wanted to know next. 'How did you learn this magic?'

Monkey gave them an unexpurgated version of his travels – including Subodhi's imparting of immortality.

'What luck!' applauded the monkeys, toasting their king with bowls of coconut-and-grape wine, divine flowers and fruit.

Chapter Three

After Monkey's triumphal homecoming, he taught the little monkeys how to sharpen bamboo sticks into spears and file wood into knives; how to set out flags and banners; how to patrol, advance, retreat, and pitch camp. But after playing at war for a while, he mused: 'What if we really had to go into battle? What if humans or birds or beasts accused us of plotting to rebel, and raised an army to destroy us? Armed only with bamboo poles and wooden swords, how could we fight them? We must have proper swords and spears.'

'You are indeed farsighted,' the other monkeys chattered. 'But where can we get such things?'

Four monkey elders – two red-buttocked females and two long-armed apes – now stepped forward with a suggestion. 'Easily done. East of this mountain, across two hundred miles of water, lies the frontier of Aolai. There, a king rules over a city with a huge army; he must have craftsmen skilled in all kinds of metalwork. You could get weapons there,

Your Majesty, then teach us how to use them to protect ourselves forever.'

Monkey thought this a wonderful idea. 'Off you go and play,' he told his subjects. 'I'll be back soon.'

With one cloud-somersault, he crossed the two hundred miles of water in a split second and approached a densely populated city with wide streets, large marketplaces, and thousands of houses.

'This place must be awash with weapons,' he mused. 'I suppose I could go and buy them. But stealing them through sorcery would be better.' Making a sign and reciting a spell, he inhaled deeply, then blew out a gale that scoured the city with a sandstorm. Rulers and subjects fled inside their houses and bolted their doors shut. With the coast cleared, Monkey landed his cloud and rushed through the palace gate straight to the armory. There he found vast stores of every kind of weapon: knives, spears, swords, halberds, battle-axes, bows, arrows, and so on. 'But how am I to get all this home? Time for some more body division, I think.' Plucking out another handful of hairs, he once more chewed them to a pulp, then spat them out, recited a magic spell, and shouted, 'Change!' The fragments of hair turned into one hundred thousand little monkeys, all grabbing at weapons. After emptying the armory, they jumped back onto the cloud and Monkey carried them home on another gale.

Monkey King Makes Havoc in Heaven

Busy playing outside the cave when this army suddenly roared up, the Flower-Fruit monkeys fled for cover. Monkey promptly retrieved his hairs and made a pile of weapons. 'Come and choose!' he shouted to his subjects, who ran back out to learn what was going on. Once Monkey had explained his latest marvel, the crowd of monkeys spent the rest of the day playing with their new toys.

The next day, after their usual marching drill, Monkey summoned them together and made a roll call of forty-seven thousand monkey soldiers. The size of this army awed the mountain's many wild beasts: its wolves, snakes, tigers, leopards, mouse-deer, roe deer, river deer, foxes, badgers, lions, elephants, bears, antelope, wild boar, mountain oxen, gazelles, and green rhinoceroses. Every demon king from the mountain's seventy-two caves came to pay homage to the monkey king. Each year they presented tribute – golden drums, colorful flags, helmets – and answered Monkey's summons. Some provided military service; others supplies. Together, they turned Flower-Fruit Mountain into a fortress of formidable military discipline.

One day, though, Monkey had a thought. 'While you are all very quick now with all kinds of weapons, I'm finding this cutlass of mine very cumbersome.'

The four wise monkeys again stepped forward. 'You

are an immortal, Your Majesty. Ordinary weapons are not the thing for you. Can you travel underwater?'

'I have mastered seventy-two transformations,' explained Monkey. 'I can cloud-somersault, turn invisible, and apparate. I can soar to heaven and bore down into the earth. I can saunter across the sun and the moon without casting a shadow; I can pass through metal and stone. Water cannot drown me, fire cannot burn me. Is there anything I can't do?'

'Marvelous. For the water beneath this iron bridge flows directly to the palace of the dragon king of the Eastern Ocean. Why don't you go and ask him for a weapon?'

Monkey thought this an excellent plan. 'Back soon.'

Bouncing onto the bridge, he invoked the magic of aquatic restriction, then threw himself into the water, which obligingly parted for him, and headed straight to the bottom of the Eastern Ocean. Along the way he met a sea-spirit patrol, who asked him his name so that he could be announced to the dragon king. 'I am Monkey, the immortal sage of Flower-Fruit Mountain and a close neighbor of your king. I'm frankly surprised you need to ask.'

As soon as the patrol reported Monkey's arrival to the Water-Crystal Palace, the Dragon King Aoguang mustered a welcoming party of his sons, grandsons,

Monkey King Makes Havoc in Heaven

prawn soldiers, and crab generals to greet their visitor. Once they had all processed back inside the palace for formal introductions, and tea had been served, the dragon king asked Monkey about himself: how he learned the Way and what powers it had given him.

'My body is birthless and deathless,' Monkey informed him. 'I've taught my subjects to defend our cave in the mountains, but find myself without a decent weapon. I understand that my honorable neighbor here has far more magic weapons than he can possibly use, so I've come to ask for one.'

Sensing this was not a request he could refuse, the dragon king immediately ordered one of his commanders (who happened to be a perch) to present Monkey with a large cutlass.

'Not really my thing,' Monkey demurred. 'Try me with something else.'

The dragon king next ordered another subordinate, one Captain Mackerel, to bring out a nine-pronged fork with the help of an eel porter.

Monkey picked it up, then set it down again. 'Too light!'

'But it weighs 3,600 pounds,' the Dragon King pointed out, laughing. Monkey wanted nothing to do with it. By now, the dragon king was starting to feel distinctly uneasy about his uninvited guest. He asked Commander Bream and Brigadier Carp to bring out a vast halberd weighing 7,200 pounds.

After trying out a few moves, Monkey plunged it into the ground between them. 'Flimsy!'

'This is the heaviest weapon in the palace,' protested the unnerved dragon king.

'Think I was born yesterday?' Monkey giggled. 'Everyone knows the Dragon King Aoguang's not short of treasures. Go and have a proper look around your armory. If I see something I like, I'll give you a fair price.'

Just as the dragon king was reaching his wit's end, the dragon queen and her daughter slipped out from behind the throne. 'This monkey is clearly not someone to be trifled with,' they whispered to the king. 'How about giving him the magic iron from the Heavenly River? These last few days, it's been glowing mysteriously and exuding propitious vapors. A sign, perhaps?'

The dragon king said, 'But that's the measure that Yu the Great used to tame the floods, to fix the depths of rivers and seas. What good will it do this monkey?'

'Who cares?' said the queen. 'Just hand it over and get rid of him.' Seeing her point, the dragon king told Monkey about his wife's suggestion.

'I'll take a look,' conceded Monkey. 'Bring it out.'

'You'll need to view it in its current resting place,'

Monkey King Makes Havoc in Heaven

the dragon king explained. 'It's too heavy to lift.' He led his demanding visitor into the ocean treasury, from which myriad golden rays were emanating. The king pointed: 'That's it.'

Monkey went over to investigate. It was a radiant iron pillar, more than fifty feet tall* and as thick as a barrel. 'It's got potential,' he mused. 'A little too wide and a little too long, though.' The moment he said this, the pillar grew several feet shorter and several inches thinner. 'Smaller!' he commanded. It promptly shrank some more. The delighted Monkey now took it out of the treasury to examine it properly: it was a black iron rod, weighing 13,500 pounds, with a golden ring on either end. An inscription next to one of the rings read: OBEDIENT GOLDEN-HOOPED STAFF. 'A weapon that will do my bidding!' exulted Monkey. 'Smaller still!' he commanded, tossing the iron from hand to hand. It now shrank to twenty feet long, and to the diameter of a rice bowl.

As Monkey lunged, parried, and twirled his way back into the Water-Crystal Palace, the dragon king and his princes trembled with fear. Turtles and

---

* The original here says 'more than twenty feet,' but given how much shrinking Monkey subjects the iron to over the ensuing sentences, at the end of which the staff is about twenty feet long, I judged that the first number had to be an error, and therefore increased it to fifty.

tortoises retreated into their shells, while fish, shrimp, and crabs all fled for cover. 'Thanks, worthy neighbor,' Monkey said, beaming at the dragon king while inviting himself to sit back down in the throne hall.

'Don't mention it,' quavered his host.

'This lump of iron isn't bad,' Monkey continued. 'Not bad at all. But I do have one further request.'

'You do?'

'Now that I've adopted this magic staff, I feel rather underdressed. If you could rustle up some armor to go with it, I'd be much obliged.'

'I'm most dreadfully sorry, but I don't have anything suitable.'

'I don't want to be a bother to someone else. I'll sit out here till you come up with the goods.'

'I suggest you try another ocean. You might have more luck there.'

'But I've settled in so nicely here. If you're sure you don't have anything for me to wear, perhaps you'd like me to test out my new staff on you.'

'Desist, I beg you!' yelped the dragon king. 'Perhaps my brothers Aoqin in the Southern Ocean, Aoshun in the Northern Ocean, and Aorun in the Western Ocean could dig something up.'

'Too far!' Monkey declared. 'As the saying goes: a dragon king in the hand is worth three in the bush.'

'Of course,' stammered the dragon king. 'No need

at all for you to go there yourself. I will summon them immediately with my iron drum and golden bell.'

'What are you waiting for?'

Moments after the alligator general had struck the bell and the turtle marshal beaten the drum, the three dragon brothers converged on the entrance to the Water-Crystal Palace. Aoguang hurried out to meet them.

'What emergency did you bring us here for?' Aoqin asked his older brother.

'It's like this,' Aoguang replied. 'Earlier today, a so-called immortal sage from Flower-Fruit Mountain, claiming to be a neighbor of mine, turned up demanding a weapon. I finally managed to fob him off with the magic iron pillar from the Heavenly River, but he's now refusing to leave until I give him some armor, too. I don't have a thing to give him, which is why I called you here. Do you have anything that will do, so that I can get rid of him?'

'Let's call up our armies and apprehend him!' spluttered the outraged Aoqin.

'Hopeless,' Aoguang countered. 'One tap of that magic iron will finish us all.'

Aorun argued for the path of least resistance: 'Let's find him some armor, send him on his way, then make a formal complaint to Heaven, which can punish him as it sees fit.'

'Good plan,' chimed Aoshun. 'I have here a pair of cloud-hopping shoes in lotus-colored silk.'

'And I happen to have with me a golden chain-mail cuirass,' added Aorun.

'I can throw in a purple-gold phoenix-feather cap,' offered Aoqin.

Delighted, Aoguang now ushered them into the palace to meet his unruly visitor. Monkey put on his shoes, his chain-mail cuirass, and his helmet and mock-fought his way out of the palace with his iron staff, yelling 'Sorry for the trouble' as he went. Most unsettled by the whole encounter, the four dragons embarked upon a consultation process about lodging an official complaint with the Heavenly authorities. But we need not concern ourselves with that for the time being.

Parting the waters again, Monkey swept back onto the iron bridge, where his subjects were eagerly awaiting his return. When they saw their king suddenly leap out of the waves, perfectly dry and in his glittering new costume, they kneeled in awe. Monkey sat triumphantly on his throne with the iron staff propped up before him. Not knowing any better, his monkeys crowded around, anxious to try it themselves. Like dragonflies trying to shake a tree, they couldn't move it even a fraction of an inch.

Monkey King Makes Havoc in Heaven

'How did Your Majesty carry it all the way here?' they chattered in wonder.

'Every object has its master,' said Monkey, smiling and picking it up. 'For thousands of years, this piece of iron lay in the ocean treasury fixing the depth of the Heavenly River until, a few days ago, it began giving off light. It has a name – the Obedient Golden-Hooped Staff – and it does whatever I say. When I first laid eyes on it, it was fifty feet long and as thick as a barrel, but it shrank as soon as I told it to. Stand to one side, while I tell it to transform. Smaller!' In an instant, the staff had shrunk to the size of an embroidery needle, which Monkey tucked inside his ear.

'More magic!' bayed the amazed monkeys.

Their king placed the staff on the palm of his hand: 'Bigger!' he shouted. It immediately became a twenty-foot pillar that was a couple of feet in diameter. Monkey now tried a touch of cosmic imitation. Bounding out of the cave, he cried 'Grow!' and promptly shot up to one hundred thousand feet tall. His head resembled the craggy summit of Mount Tai, with flashing eyes and a butcher's-bowl mouth full of razor teeth. His staff reached up to the thirty-third story of Heaven, and down to the eighteenth level of Hell. Tigers, leopards, wolves, snakes, and the demon kings of the seventy-two caves all emerged to kowtow in terror. A moment later, Monkey undid the magic, shrank the staff down to the size of a needle, tucked it inside his ear again, and sashayed back inside the cave.

The assembled company now sat down to a magnificent banquet, amid fluttering banners and banging gongs. After feasting on a hundred delicacies, all washed down with coconut and grape wine, they returned to their military training. Monkey promoted his four wise monkeys: the two red-buttocked females were named marshals, the long-armed apes generals, in charge of building fortifications, pitching camp, and distributing rewards and punishments. With the day-to-day business thus taken care of, Monkey spent his days riding mist and clouds, sauntering over oceans, and touring mountains. His displays of magic made him powerful, talented friends. He swore brotherhood with six great kings: Bull Demon, Dragon-Monster, Roc-Fiend, Lion-Camel, Macaque, and Giant-Ape. Every day they gathered in Water-Curtain Cave, discussing civil and military affairs over cups of wine, singing, dancing, roaming the world, and living their best lives.

One day, Monkey instructed his four commanders to arrange a banquet for the seven brothers: oxen and horses were slaughtered, sacrifices were offered to heaven and earth, assorted imps were ordered to sing and dance, and everyone proceeded to get thoroughly drunk. After seeing his six compadres off, Monkey lay down under the shade of a pine tree and, a moment later, nodded off, surrounded by a hushed, protective circle of his subjects. As he slept, Monkey dreamed that two silent individuals, holding an official summons on which his full name – Sun Wukong – was written, tied him up and lugged him to the edge of a city. Still groggy with drink, Monkey half discerned an iron sign: WELCOME TO HELL. This brought him to his senses. 'Why have you dragged me to the Kingdom of Death?' he demanded.

'You've reached the end of your allotted span,' his escorts informed him. 'Our orders are to bring you here.'

Monkey was outraged: 'I have transcended the Three Realms and the Five Phases and am no longer under King Yama's jurisdiction. Why has your idiot sovereign had me arrested?'

Ignoring the protest, the two soul-policemen went on trying to pull him inside. Now in a proper fury, Monkey pulled the magic iron staff out from behind his ear. With one wave, it grew into a cudgel, and Monkey smashed his guards to a pulp. He untied himself and charged into the city, spinning his staff this way and that. Bull-headed and horse-faced demons fled in terror, while ghost soldiers rushed to alert the Palace of Hell. 'Disaster, Your Majesties!'

they reported. 'An outrageous monkey is about to smash his way into the palace!'

Thoroughly alarmed, the ten kings of the Underworld went out to investigate. 'Tell us your name,' they called to the furious Monkey.

'How dare you not know who I am?' raged Monkey. 'How dare you have me arrested?'

'A – a clerical error, perhaps,' the infernal kings replied falteringly.

'Know then,' thundered Monkey, 'that I am Sun Wukong, Heaven-born sage of Water-Curtain Cave on Flower-Fruit Mountain. Now who the hell are you?'

The ten kings bowed. 'We are the emperors of darkness, the ten underworld kings of the wheel of karma.'

'Tell me your names or I'll beat you senseless.' They did not withhold the information. 'Well, if you're all such powerful kings, with superior intellects and the like, how can you have made such a mistake? For I, Monkey, have learned the Way of Immortality and will live as long as Heaven itself. What business do you have with me?'

'Calm yourself,' soothed the kings. 'Lots of people have the same surname as you. It's probably a simple case of mistaken identity.'

'Rubbish!' Monkey retorted. 'The warrant never

Monkey King Makes Havoc in Heaven

lies. I want to see the register of births and deaths this very minute.'

The ten kings invited him into the palace to take a look.

Keeping a firm hold on his staff, Monkey sat himself down in the middle of the palace, while the ten kings ordered a judge from the records department to produce the ledgers for his perusal. The legal official scuttled off and soon returned with a pile of volumes, including the registers for the ten species of living creatures. Monkey went through them one by one: the register of the hairless and the short-haired; the hairy; the feathered; the crawling; and the scaly – no mention of our Monkey. Monkey, you see, was hard to classify. He shared some points of resemblance with humans, but not enough to be categorized alongside them; though his hair was on the short side, he did not belong to the kingdom of the hairless and the short-haired; although he was animal-like in appearance, he did not answer to the unicorn; though he was known to fly, he was not accountable to the phoenix. He was eventually located in his own separate ledger, which Monkey personally examined, finding his name under the entry for Soul Number 1350, with the clarification: 'Stone monkey born of Heaven. Lifespan: 342 years. A good death.' 'I can't remember how old I actually am,' Monkey said. 'I just want to delete my name.

Pass me a brush.' The judge quickly found one and loaded it with ink, and Monkey crossed out not only his name but also every name in the monkey section of the ledgers. 'So that's that,' he announced, tossing the register away. 'So long!' And he smashed his way back out of Hell. Glad to keep as great a distance as possible between themselves and Monkey, the ten kings agreed to consult the Pope of Darkness, in his residence in the Emerald Cloud Palace, about filing a formal complaint in Heaven.

As he bashed his way out of the infernal city, Monkey tripped on a clump of grass. Suddenly waking up, he realized it had all been a dream. 'How much did you drink at the banquet?' his subjects asked him as he stretched. 'You slept through till morning.' Monkey told them what had happened in his dream and how he had persuaded the kings of the underworld to cross all their names off the ledger of death, at which news his subjects kowtowed with ecstatic gratitude. And from that point on, most mountain monkeys never got old, for the Underworld no longer had their names and addresses.

Let us turn now to the court of the Jade Emperor, where – at the morning session in the Hall of Divine Mists in the Golden-Turreted Cloud Palace – a Taoist immortal named Qiu Hongji had just stepped out of the ranks of the Heavenly ministers and announced the arrival of the Dragon King Aoguang, to present a memorial. Bidding him enter, the Jade Emperor read the petition handed to him by a page boy:

> Your unworthy subject Aoguang begs to inform his imperial eminence that a bogus immortal of Water-Curtain Cave on Flower-Fruit Mountain, by the name of Sun Wukong (also known as Monkey), has been harassing this small, weak dragon. He broke into my palace, demanded a weapon using threats of grievous bodily harm, then again used intimidation to extort a suit of armor. He terrorized my watery relatives and sundry turtles and alligators. After presenting him with a magic iron staff, a golden phoenix-feather helmet, a suit of chain-mail, and cloud-shoes, my brothers and I – dragon kings, all – saw him off with all due courtesy. But still he terrorized us with magic and violence and didn't say a proper thank you. As we ourselves are no match for him, we respectfully beg you to apprehend this demon to restore peace and prosperity to the ocean bed. Humbly yours, etc., etc.

'You may return to your ocean,' the Jade Emperor replied. 'We'll deal with this miscreant.' Bowing his head in thanks, the dragon king departed.

Directly afterward, further visitors were announced: 'The Minister of Hell and the Pope of Darkness also wish to present a memorial.' This time the Jade Girl, the emperor's director of communications, delivered the document to the emperor. It went like this:

> Heaven is for gods and earth for ghosts; birth and death proceed cyclically, for such is the immutable order of nature. Today, however, a Heaven-born demonic monkey, one Sun Wukong of Water-Curtain Cave on Flower-Fruit Mountain, ferociously resisted arrest. He beat to death two spectral policemen and traumatized the ten Merciful Kings of Hell. After making the most awful fuss in the Infernal Palace, he forced us to erase his name on the register of death and banned us from arresting any of his monkey relatives, thereby making a shambles of the wheel of reincarnation. I humbly beg you to subdue this demon and restore peace and security in the Underworld. Respectfully yours, etc., etc.

'You may return to the Underworld,' the Jade Emperor pronounced. 'We'll deal with this miscreant.' The hellish heads of state retired, with thanks.

His Celestial Majesty now questioned his officials

Monkey King Makes Havoc in Heaven

about this infamous monkey. 'When was he born, and when did he start making trouble like this? How has he become so powerful?'

'This creature,' related Thousand-Mile Eye and Follow-the-Wind Ear, 'began life some three hundred years ago as a stone monkey born of Heaven. After a perfectly ordinary start in life, he somehow learned the Way of Immortality and is now able to terrorize dragons and tigers and bully the Underworld into deleting him from their ledgers of death.'

'So which,' responded the Jade Emperor, 'of my divine generals will descend to earth to capture him?'

'Majesty,' the Spirit of Longevity from Venus ventured, 'given that this monkey is a child of heaven and earth, of the sun and the moon, that he walks on two feet, and has attained immortality, I propose that we treat him as we would a human. I humbly suggest you offer him an amnesty, summon him to Heaven and give him a government job. Once he's inside the system, he'll have to behave. If he accepts, we can bamboozle him with sinecures; if he refuses, we can apprehend him. In any case, such a strategy will save us a military campaign and bring an unruly immortal to heel.'

'Excellent!' rejoiced the Jade Emperor, ordering a nearby constellation to scribble out the amnesty and appointing the Gold Star of Venus as his peace envoy.

Wu Cheng'en

Landing his auspicious cloud in front of Water-Curtain Cave, Gold Star announced himself and his mission to the crowd of monkeys: 'I am the representative of the Jade Emperor, who invites your king to join the Heavenly civil service. Run along now and tell him.' The message bounced along a chain of monkey minions; by the time it reached their king deep inside the cave it had become: 'An old man outside with a piece of paper on his back says come up to Heaven.'

'Ha!' exclaimed Monkey. 'I was just thinking the other day how much I'd like to do that. Send him in!' Once inside, Gold Star introduced himself formally and repeated his invitation. 'Don't mind if I do, chum!' said Monkey, beaming. 'But let's feast first.'

'As I'm on imperial business,' protested Gold Star, 'I daren't delay. Let us ascend to Heaven directly. Once the Jade Emperor has given you your Very Important Job, we'll have plenty of time to chat.'

'Sorry you'll leave empty-bellied.' Monkey shrugged and called his four generals over: 'Keep the little monkeys at their training. Meantime, I'll have a sniff around Heaven and see whether you can all come, too.' He then hopped onto Gold Star's personal cloud, and they rose into the sky.

Chapter Four

Thanks to Monkey's exceptional skill at cloud-somersaulting, he soon left Gold Star far behind him and arrived first at the South Gate of Heaven. But when he tried to enter, his way was blocked by the spears, swords, and halberds of nine gold-armored divine warriors guarding the entrance. 'That Gold Star's a fraud!' griped an outraged Monkey. 'He told me I was an honored guest!' At this moment, the panting Gold Star caught up. 'You told me the Jade Emperor was going to give me an amnesty,' Monkey railed at him. 'So why are these goons blocking my way?'

'Calm down,' Gold Star soothed, laughing. 'As this is your first time in Heaven, our guards have no idea who you are. They daren't let just anyone in. Once you've met the Jade Emperor, been officially registered as an immortal, and given a government job, you can come and go as you please.'

'I'm not going,' Monkey said sulkily.

'Come on,' said Gold Star, yanking him toward

the gate. 'Let us through, Guardians!' he called out. 'I bring with me, on the orders of the Jade Emperor, an immortal from the world below.' When the guards stepped back, lowering their weapons, Monkey decided to trust Gold Star and walked slowly in through the green-tiled, jade-studded portal.

Heaven, Monkey had to admit, was quite something. Rainbows of golden light shimmered through purple mists, evergreen grasses, and ever-blooming flowers. Multicolored phoenixes soared around the thirty-three palaces, while the seventy-two ceremonial halls teemed with jade unicorns. The inner halls were propped up by huge pillars coiled with scarlet-whiskered, gold-scaled dragons. Officials glittering with gold and precious stones rustled back and forth in robes of crimson gauze. When the drums of Heaven sounded, Monkey followed ten thousand courtiers through a gold-studded jade door to the emperor's throne room, the Hall of Divine Mists. Topped by extravagantly decorated eaves and ferocious-looking carved animal guardians, the hall was roofed by a vast, brilliant dome of purple-gold, beneath which goddesses fluttered fans and crystal platters were heaped with elixirs. Earth paled in comparison.

Gold Star led Monkey directly up to an audience with the emperor. While his escort was busy prostrating himself, Wukong stood disrespectfully upright. 'In accordance with the emperor's decree,' announced Gold Star, 'I bring you the bogus immortal.'

'And he is . . . ?' asked the Jade Emperor.

'You're looking at him!' Monkey now piped up, finally making a perfunctory bow.

The attendant officials paled in horror. 'What a savage!' they murmured. 'Death's too good for him.'

'The bogus immortal,' the Jade Emperor pronounced, 'has not yet learned manners. We will pardon him this time.' Next, the emperor asked if there were any staff vacancies that Monkey could fill. A Star Spirit from Immortal Resources reported that while there were no openings in any of the ministries, the stables did need a supervisor. 'I hereby appoint you Imperial Groom,' announced the Jade Emperor. The assembled courtiers chorused their thanks, while Monkey whooped his. The emperor then dispatched the Star Spirit of Jupiter to escort Monkey to the stables to take up his new appointment.

Elated at his latest professional development, Monkey began by taking his duties very seriously. He gathered together his team (administrators, accountants, stable hands) and made a detailed survey of the current state of stable management. There were, he inventoried, a thousand heavenly horses, made up of thirty-three extraordinary breeds (Wind Chasers,

Distance Devourers, Light Leapers, Red Rabbits, and the like), all with thunderous gallops and inexhaustible stamina for riding mist and clouds. Monkey painstakingly oversaw the accountants who sourced supplies; the laborers who washed, groomed, fed, and watered the horses; the deputies and assistants who kept everything else running smoothly. Monkey petted and coaxed the horses by day and watched over them by night. If they wanted to sleep, they were woken and fed; if they wanted to gallop, they were brought back to the trough. Within two weeks he had broken them all in.

One day, when all was quiet in the stables, Monkey's colleagues held a welcome banquet for their new supervisor. While the others were merrily drinking away, Monkey suddenly set down his cup. 'What grade am I in the civil service here?'

'You don't have one,' his colleagues replied.

'You mean I'm too high up for the grade system?' Monkey asked.

'Quite the opposite. You're so low-ranking you're off the bottom of the scale. You've done a famous job since starting in the stables, but you'll never get more than a grudging "not bad" from the higher-ups. If the horses lose any weight, senior management will tan your hide. And if they get injured under your watch, you'll be severely punished.'

Monkey King Makes Havoc in Heaven

'So that's what they think of Monkey!' the Imperial Groom exploded. 'Don't they know I'm the King of Flower-Fruit Mountain? How have they hoodwinked me into looking after their smelly horses? I'm off!' Pushing over his desk, he took the iron out from behind his ear, shook it out to the thickness of a cudgel, and barged his way out of the South Gate. Knowing that Monkey was now on the immortal payroll, the sentries didn't dare arrest him.

Within an instant, his cloud landed back on Flower-Fruit Mountain, where the four generals and the monstrous monarchs were busy with their usual drills. 'My children!' he cried. 'Monkey's back!'

The monkey masses swept their king back onto his throne and conjured up a feast. 'You've been in Heaven more than ten years,' they acclaimed him. 'What glories have you achieved in this time?'

'Ten years? I've been away barely a fortnight.'

'One day in Heaven,' his acolytes advised him, 'is equivalent to a year on earth. What ministry did they give you?'

'Don't ask!' Monkey waved his hands dismissively. 'That pathetic Jade Emperor is the worst – couldn't recognize genius if it punched him in the nose. He made me his groom – can you believe it? It was fun to begin with, but when my colleagues told me how low-ranking the job was, I got so mad I smashed up the lousy banquet they were holding for me and came straight back here. They can keep their rotten job.'

'Marvelous! Superb!' cried the little monkeys. 'Why would you want to look after their stinky horses when you can be king of this cave? You monkeys in the kitchen, hurry up with that welcome-home wine! Our king needs cheering up!'

In the middle of the banquet, two visitors were announced: a pair of rhinoceros-horned demon kings. As soon as Monkey had them shown in, they rushed up to prostrate themselves. 'Having heard about your Heavenly appointment and that you'd returned covered in glory, we wish to congratulate you with this red and yellow robe and to offer our faithful service.' Monkey happily slipped on the robe, accepted the adulation of the entire banqueting hall, and appointed the demon kings his frontline commanders.

'Just as a matter of interest, what post *did* Heaven give you?' the new arrivals asked.

'That crummy Jade Emperor made me his groom,' grumbled Monkey.

'What?' The demon kings seemed astonished. 'How could an omnipotent magic monkey be made to look after horses? You are the Great Sage Equal to Heaven!'

Monkey thought this was the best thing ever. 'Quick as you can,' he ordered his generals, 'make me a flag saying "The Great Sage Equal to Heaven" and mount it on a bamboo pole. No more of this "Great King" rubbish. And tell my brothers the monstrous monarchs, too.'

Back in Heaven, the following day the Heavenly Preceptor – a celestial master by the name of Zhang Daoling – led two stable administrators up to the throne. 'Your Majesty,' they reported, prostrating themselves, 'your new groom absconded from the Heavenly Palace yesterday, complaining that the job he had been given was unworthy of him.' At that very moment, the Guardians of the South Gate also appeared to report on Monkey's brusque exit.

'Back to your posts, all of you,' the Jade Emperor declared. 'We will dispatch an expedition to capture this monster.'

The Heavenly King Li Jing and his third son, Prince Nezha, immediately stepped forward. 'Your talentless subjects volunteer for this task.'

Gratified, the emperor appointed King Li his Monster-Quashing Marshal and ordered father and son to enlist an army to descend to the realm below.

The two immortals turned their palace into the campaign headquarters, where they appointed a god named Mighty-Spirit to direct the frontline operations, General Fish-Belly to bring up the rear, and the Commander of Sprites to maintain troop morale. The force passed out of the South Gate and headed straight for Flower-Fruit Mountain, where the immortals selected a flat stretch of terrain to make camp and told Mighty-Spirit to formally declare war. After buckling on his armor and taking up his Ax of Virtue, Mighty-Spirit approached Water-Curtain Cave, in front of which he could see crowds of horrors – wolves, snakes, tigers, leopards, and the like – leaping, roaring, and waving swords and spears.

'Damnable beasts!' bellowed Mighty-Spirit. 'Tell that stable hand of yours that the Great General of Highest Heaven has come, on the orders of the Jade Emperor, to subdue him. If he does not surrender instantly, we will annihilate the lot of you.'

'Oh, calamity!' wailed Monkey's creatures, scurrying back inside the cave.

'Whatever's wrong?' asked Monkey. His subjects repeated the gist of Mighty-Spirit's announcement. 'Bring me my fighting clothes!' he demanded. Pulling on his purple-gold helmet, his golden armor, and his cloud shoes, he seized his golden-hooped staff and led his troops out of the cave, where he positioned them for battle. Taking in Monkey's resplendent battle dress, burning eyes, and bared fangs, Mighty-Spirit had to admit that his antagonist did not look in the least ready to be subdued.

'Rude and unreasonable monkey!' roared Mighty-Spirit nonetheless. 'Do you know who I am?'

'How could I, you dim-witted deity?' Monkey shot back. 'We've never met. Identify yourself!'

'How can you not recognize me, you lying ape? Why, I am none other than Mighty-Spirit, frontline commander under Heavenly King Li Jing, from the Divine Empyrean, under orders from the Jade Emperor to bring you to heel. Take off your armor and surrender, or we will exterminate every creature on this mountain. If you put up the slightest resistance, I will instantly turn you into salted vegetable powder!'

'You're the rude and unreasonable one!' riposted Monkey. 'I'd have finished you off already if I didn't need you to take a message back for me. Run back to Heaven and tell that Jade Emperor of yours that he made a big mistake sending me to look after his mangy horses. Read this banner' – he gestured at the GREAT SAGE EQUAL TO HEAVEN notice – 'and get the measure of my genius. If your emperor gives me a promotion worthy of my abilities, I'll call off my armies and peace will reign in heaven and earth. But if he doesn't deliver, I'll make things pretty hot for him in the Hall of Divine Mists.'

Mighty-Spirit gave three scornful barks of laughter. 'You insolent ape. So now you think you're the equal of Heaven, do you? Eat my ax!' Aiming at Monkey's head, he took a massive swing, which Monkey serenely parried with his staff.

The battle was on: they clashed to the left and to the right; they confused each other by generating cloud and fog; they splattered each other with mud and sand. Although Mighty-Spirit's ax cut like a phoenix swooping through flowers, it was no match for the iron staff that the self-styled Great Sage whirled about him. Monkey took advantage of Mighty-Spirit's exhaustion to aim a direct blow to his adversary's head; though Mighty-Spirit blocked it, his ax handle split from the impact and he fled the battlefield. 'Useless pustule!' crowed Monkey after him. 'I'll let you live this time, but mind you pass on my message! Get a move on!'

Returning to camp, Mighty-Spirit kneeled before King Li. 'This stable hand has quite some powers,' he panted. 'I'm afraid I was unable to defeat him.'

'You're a disgrace!' raged the king. 'Off with your head!'

'Calm yourself, Father,' advised Nezha. 'Let me go and get the measure of this monkey.'

Allowing himself to be swayed, King Li banished Mighty-Spirit to await court-martial, while Nezha strapped on his armor and charged off to Water-Curtain Cave, where he interrupted Monkey in the middle of dismissing his troops. Nezha's baby face belied his prowess as a warrior; he was extraordinarily agile – able to fly, leap, and transform at will – and was armed, moreover, with six magic weapons.

'Who's this dumpling?' Monkey asked. 'What business do you have with me?'

'Monstrous monkey!' shouted Nezha. 'How dare you not recognize me? For I am Prince Nezha, third son of Heavenly King Li. I am here on the orders of the Jade Emperor to capture you.'

This made Monkey laugh a good deal. 'Does your mother know you're out, little princeykins? How many baby teeth have you lost already? I'll spare you this time – for the sake of your adorable chubby cheeks. Just read the banner – if you've learned to read yet – and tell the Jade Emperor to give me a proper job. If he gives me a promotion, I'll forget we got off to such a bad start. If not, I'll take my quarrel to the emperor's own throne room. And I'll be bringing my staff, too.'

Reading the banner, Nezha was even more provoked. 'Extraordinary impudence! Prepare for a pounding!'

'Fine by me,' said Monkey nonchalantly. 'Swing away.'

The furious Nezha turned into a monster with three heads and six arms, each holding a different weapon: a demon-beheading sword, a demon-hacking knife, a demon-strangling rope, a demon-taming pestle, a wheel of fire, and an embroidered ball. Witnessing this transformation, Wukong did feel a slight twinge of alarm. 'So this whippersnapper has a few tricks up his six sleeves. Nothing to worry about, though. Time for a little monkey magic.' Monkey also became a creature of three heads and six arms; his golden-hooped staff divided into three, one for each pair of hands. After no clear victor emerged from the initial clashes, the prince multiplied his six weapons into tens of thousands; Monkey did the same with his staffs. The local monstrous monarchs scurried inside their caves and slammed their doors behind them.

After thirty rounds, though, Monkey's quick wits prevailed: in the thick of the fight, he pulled out a strand of hair and transformed it into a perfect likeness of himself. While Nezha was fooled by the specious Monkey, the real one leaped up from behind and hit him hard on the left arm. Reeling from the unexpected blow, Nezha turned and fled back to the camp.

Having seen everything from the front of his battle formation, King Li was about to rush into the fray himself when Nezha pulled him back. 'This stable hand *does* know a thing or two about fighting. He even managed to wound me on the shoulder.'

'How can we possibly defeat him?' Nezha's father quailed.

'He's planted a banner outside his cave, declaring that he is the Great Sage Equal to Heaven,' explained Nezha. 'If the emperor gives him that job, he says he'll agree to a truce. If not, he'll take his fight to the emperor's throne room.'

'Let's pass his ultimatum on to the emperor,' King Li ruled. 'We can always send in reinforcements if the emperor's against détente.'

Meanwhile, the creatures of Flower-Fruit Mountain were celebrating Monkey's famous victories with a first-rate feast. 'Now that I'm the Great Sage Equal to Heaven,' he said to his sworn brothers, 'why don't you rename yourselves, too?'

'Good idea!' exclaimed King Bull Demon. 'I'll call myself Great Sage Parallel with Heaven.' Dragon-Monster opted for Ocean-Covering Great Sage, Roc-Fiend for Heaven-Merging Great Sage, Lion-Camel for Mountain-Moving Great Sage, Macaque for Fast-as-the-Wind Great Sage, and Giant-Ape for God-Routing Great Sage. For at that moment, these seven monsters could call themselves – and do – exactly what they pleased. After a day of revelry, each retired to his cave.

Meanwhile, King Li and Prince Nezha were reporting on the war to the Jade Emperor. 'We were, in truth, surprised by the abilities of this monkey and beg for more soldiers to destroy him.'

'How powerful can one monkey be,' wondered the Jade Emperor, 'that reinforcements are required?'

'We apologize for our treacherous failure, but this demonic monkey's iron staff first defeated Mighty-Spirit,' Nezha explained, 'then wounded me on the arm.' He next reported Monkey's demand for a promotion.

'Outrageous!' snapped the Jade Emperor. 'Have him executed forthwith!'

Gold Star now stepped forward. 'This baneful monkey knows how to bluster, but not when to stop. I suspect that even if we commit more troops, he won't be easily defeated, and the campaign will exhaust our armies. Why doesn't Your Majesty bring him around with another amnesty and give him an honorary title?'

'What sort of thing do you have in mind?' the emperor asked.

'Let him call himself Great Sage Equal to Heaven – a non-stipendiary post with no duties. That way, we'll keep him tame and tethered here, and peace will be restored.'

'Very well,' agreed the emperor, and dispatched Gold Star with a second amnesty.

Heading straight for Water-Curtain Cave, Gold Star found the area somewhat changed. The entire mountain was thick with every species of monster, armed to the teeth and spitting with aggression. As soon as they saw Gold Star, they made as if to attack him. 'Chieftains,' the shaken envoy placated them, 'please tell your Great Sage that I come from the Jade Emperor with a special invitation.'

The crowd of demons pelted into the cave to report to Monkey: 'That old man from up above's back with another invite.'

'And not a moment too soon!' exclaimed Monkey. 'They treated me shabbily before, but I expect they've learned their lesson now.' He told his lieutenants to wave banners and beat drums and generally put on a good show for their visitor. Pulling his red and yellow robe on over his armor, Monkey led his followers to the mouth of the cave. 'In you come, old chap!' he hailed Gold Star, who immediately followed Monkey inside.

'I understand,' Gold Star began, 'that because the Great Sage felt his previous posting was unworthy of him, he went absent without leave from the imperial stables. But all officials have to start at the bottom and rise through the ranks, so you really had no reason to complain. After you defeated Nezha, the prince reported back to the Jade Emperor that you wished to be appointed Great Sage Equal to Heaven. The other generals wouldn't hear of it, but I stuck my neck out for you and persuaded the emperor to invite you back to take up your Great Sageship. What do you say?'

'Thanks ever so!' Monkey beamed. 'And sorry for all the trouble. But are you sure it'll go through?'

'I had the title approved before I left. Any problems this time, you can take them up with me directly.'

Gold Star once more refused Monkey's offer of a banquet, and the two of them headed back to Heaven on a cloud. The Guardians of the South Gate this time welcomed Monkey with hands folded in front of their chests, and he and Gold Star entered the Hall of Divine Mists. 'As ordered,' announced Gold Star, prostrating himself, 'I have brought the rebellious stable hand back.'

'I hereby proclaim you "Great Sage Equal to Heaven,"' the emperor told Monkey. 'But this time, behave.' Monkey gave a huge whoop of thanks, and the Jade Emperor ordered two officials from the maintenance department to build the new appointment a mansion to the right of the Orchard of

Immortal Peaches. The palace was to house two optimistically named departments – the Ministries of Peace and Quiet and of the Spirit of Calm. The emperor deputized a handful of Taoist deities to serve as Monkey's aides, gifted him with two bottles of imperial wine and ten gold flowers, and ordered him to work on his self-control. Monkey retreated to his palace, where he promptly opened the bottles of wine and drank the lot with his new colleagues. Then, after seeing them all off back to their own palaces, he settled down to live exactly as he pleased.

But did he live happily ever after? Read on to find out.

Chapter Five

Now we must remind you that the Great Sage Equal to Heaven was, when all was said and done, still a monkey demon. He had no idea about rank or salary – all he knew, or cared about, was that he was on the Heavenly Register of Officials. His departmental aides waited on him hand and foot, day and night; as long as he got three square meals and a good night's sleep, he was happy. In his unlimited free time, he cloud-toured other palaces and grew friendly with a constellation of heavenly luminaries: stars, generals, and guardians.

Monkey's burgeoning social network did not go unnoticed, and one morning at court a Taoist immortal brought it to the attention of the Jade Emperor. 'With nothing else to occupy him, the Great Sage Equal to Heaven has taken to hobnobbing with stars. All this overfamiliarity and indolence, I fear, will lead to trouble, and erode hierarchy and order. He needs to be given something to do, to keep him out of mischief.'

Monkey King Makes Havoc in Heaven

The Jade Emperor immediately summoned Monkey, who bounded amiably into the throne room. 'Have you got a treat for me? A promotion, perhaps?'

'I understand,' the Jade Emperor told him, 'that you have too much time on your hands. So I'm going to give you a job. From now on, you're the caretaker of the Orchard of Immortal Peaches. Don't mess up.'

Monkey gave his time-honored whoop of thanks and left.

Eager to get started, he went straight into the orchard but was soon stopped by a local gardening spirit, who wanted to know what he was doing there. 'The Jade Emperor's just put me in charge, so I'm here to get the measure of the place.' Immediately saluting his new superior, the spirit summoned the orchard's staff – the maintenance staff who weeded between the trees, watered and pruned them, and swept up the leaves – to give him a tour.

A wonderful sight awaited Monkey. Each tree – personally planted by the Queen Mother of the Jade Pool – was smothered in deep pink blossoms and groaned with golden fruit. 'There are thirty-six hundred trees in total,' the spirit explained. 'The front group of twelve hundred bear small flowers and fruit. Their fruit ripen once every three thousand years. Anyone who eats one will become an immortal, with a light, strong body. The twelve hundred in the middle bear dense flowers and sweet fruit. Their fruit ripen once every six thousand years. Anyone who eats one will float up to Heaven and never grow old. The twelve hundred at the back bear fruit with purple veins and pale yellow stones, ripening once every nine thousand years. Anyone who eats one will live as long as heaven and earth, the sun and the moon.' Delighted by his new workplace, Monkey inspected all the trees and pavilions before returning home. Every three days or so he visited to enjoy the scenery, and entirely gave up his footloose socializing.

One day, noticing that more than half the peaches on the older trees had ripened, he grew desperate to try them. But because his personal aides and the immortal gardeners were always close by, there was never a convenient moment to snaffle one – until a plan suddenly came to him. 'Wait outside for me, would you?' he asked them. 'I feel like taking a nap in this pavilion.' Once his immortal attendants had retreated, Monkey scampered up a large tree and devoured as many of the biggest, ripest, juiciest peaches as he wanted (not a small number). He then jumped down and summoned his retinue to escort him home. Every few days, he would gorge himself on peaches, using the same ruse.

Monkey King Makes Havoc in Heaven

Time passed in this delicious way until one morning the Queen Mother decided to host a Great Grand Festival of Immortal Peaches in her Palace of the Jade Pool and ordered her immortal ladies-in-waiting – Red Gown, Blue Gown, White Gown, Black Gown, Purple Gown, Yellow Gown, and Green Gown – to pick peaches for the event. As they approached the orchard gate, they spotted the local spirit, his gardeners, and Monkey's aides standing outside and explained the purpose of their visit. 'Hold on,' the spirit replied. 'There's been a change of management around here. The Jade Emperor has put the Great Sage Equal to Heaven in charge and we have to report to him before opening the gate.'

'Where is he right now?' asked one of the ladies.

'Inside, napping in a pavilion.'

'Then we'll go and find him. We mustn't keep our mistress waiting.'

The spirit escorted them in, but only Monkey's robe and cap were to be found inside the pavilion – for after removing them to climb up and pilfer a few peaches, our Great Sage had shrunk himself to two inches tall and was busy snoozing amid the dense foliage at the crown of a tree. 'What should we do?' asked one of the ladies.

'The Great Sage often wanders off,' advised one of his aides. 'He must have left to meet a friend. You go ahead and pick your peaches; we'll let him know you were here.' Weaving in and out of the trees, the ladies-in-waiting managed to pick two baskets from the trees at the front and three from the middle rows, but there were hardly any peaches on the trees at the back – and these thin pickings were green and hard, for of course Monkey had eaten all the ripe fruit.

After a long, hard search, they finally spotted a red and white peach on a south-facing branch. Green Gown pulled it near, then – after Red Gown had picked the fruit – let the branch snap back into position. As chance would have it, tiny Monkey had been sleeping on that very branch, and the twanging motion startled him awake. He instantly grew back to his normal size, pulled the iron out from behind his ear, and grew it to the thickness of a cudgel. 'How dare you steal my peaches, you disgusting fiends!' he roared.

The seven ladies huddled together in terror. 'Don't be angry, Great Sage,' they begged. 'We're the Queen Mother's ladies-in-waiting. She sent us to pick peaches for her festival. Because the orchard spirit couldn't find you, we decided to get on with picking the peaches. Forgive us!'

Monkey's rage instantly melted into delight. 'Enchanting news. And who, may I ask, has the Queen Mother invited?'

'From past experience: the Buddha, the Bodhisattvas, the holy monks and the arhats of the west, Guanyin from the South Pole, the Holy Emperor of Highest Mercy from the East, the ancient immortals of the Ten Continents and Three Islands, the Dark Spirit of the North Pole, and the Great Immortal of the Yellow Horn of the Imperial Center. Then there'll be the Five Elders from the Five Quarters, the Star Spirits of the Five Poles, the Three Pure Ones, the Four Emperors, the Heavenly Deva of the Great Monad, and everyone else from the Upper Eight Caves. From the Middle Eight Caves, she'll have invited the Jade Emperor, the Nine Heroes, the Spirits of Seas and Mountains, and then the Pope of Darkness, and the Earthly Immortals from the Lower Eight Caves. Pretty much anyone who's anyone.'

'And how about me?' Monkey smiled.

'She's not mentioned you as such.'

'I am the Great Sage Equal to Heaven, you know,' explained Monkey. 'The party won't be the same without me.'

'We only know about past protocol. We don't know what will happen this time.'

'Fair enough,' said Monkey. 'You take it easy here for a bit, while I go and find out whether Monkey's on the guest list.'

Monkey made a sign with his fingers, chanted a spell, and used immobilization magic to freeze the seven ladies-in-waiting beneath the peach trees. He then hopped onto an auspicious cloud and headed straight for the Jade Pool. As he approached the venue of the Peach Festival, the Barefoot Spirit ran straight into him. A cunning plan for hoodwinking his way into the banquet immediately formed in Monkey's mind. 'Where are you going, dear Barefoot?' he asked.

'Why, to the peach banquet, of course.'

'Just as well I bumped into you, then. Knowing how fast I am at cloud-somersaulting, the Jade Emperor told me to make a circuit of all the main thoroughfares into Heaven, to tell guests to go first to a rehearsal of ceremonies in the Hall of Perfect Brightness.'

'Strange,' ruminated Barefoot. 'The rehearsal's usually at the Jade Pool. I wonder why they've changed it this year.' But because he was an honest, trusting sort of immortal, Barefoot turned his own hallowed cloud around and made for the Hall of Perfect Brightness instead.

Monkey now chanted another spell to transform himself into an exact likeness of Barefoot, landed next to the Palace of the Jade Pool, and entered with a catlike tread. The palace's ornamented interior was heavy with the most marvelous fragrances. A banqueting table – inlaid with multihued gold – was piled high with delicacies: dragon livers, phoenix marrow, bear paws, and orangutan lips. No guests had arrived yet. Just as the Great Sage was busy goggling at the scene before him, he suddenly smelled exquisitely aromatic wine. Spotting in a corridor leading off the main hall some immortal stewards distilling some alcoholic ambrosia, the Great Sage felt his monkey mouth begin to water uncontrollably; he simply had to have some. But how to get past the brewery staff? Magic was the answer, as usual. He pulled out a few of his hairs, chewed them into pieces, spat them out, recited a spell, and changed them into a swarm of nap-inducing insects. The instant they crawled over the stewards' faces, the servants crumpled to the ground and nodded off. After guzzling the choicest items from the table, Monkey skipped into the corridor and glugged to his heart's content.

Although now as drunk as a skunk, he remained lucid enough to reflect upon his actions. 'Not good! Not good at all! Once the guests arrive, they'll lay into me for spoiling their banquet. Best to go home and sleep it off.' Careening this way and that, Monkey soon took a wrong turn and found himself in front of the Heavenly Palace of Tushita – home of Laozi, the Taoist patriarch. 'How in heaven did I end up here? No matter. I've been meaning to call on Laozi for ages, and now here I am – might as well say hello.' Clattering in, he found the place deserted – for Laozi was elsewhere, giving a lecture to assembled worthies in the three-tiered Pavilion of Vermilion Mound Elixir. Heading straight for the potions room, Monkey found five calabashes suspended over a lit oven, each containing fully smelted elixir. 'Top stuff!' rejoiced Monkey. 'I've wanted to get my hands on some of this for ages. Since Laozi's not around to ask, I'll have a little taste – just for research, of course.' He tipped the contents of the gourds down his throat, as if he were gobbling up fried beans.

The elixir immediately woke him from his intoxication and enabled him to make a sober analysis of the situation. 'Bad! Very bad! If the Jade Emperor finds out about this, he'll skin me alive. What to do? Run away! Run away! Down to earth, where I'll go back to being a king.' In the interest of discretion, he chose the West Gate rather than the South Gate out of Heaven (having taken the precaution of making himself invisible first) and landed on Flower-Fruit Mountain. 'I'm back, little ones!' he announced.

The throng of monkeys and cave demons – then in the middle of their military training – dropped their weapons in surprise and kneeled. 'You were enjoying yourself so much in Heaven, you forgot all about us,' they said reproachfully.

'But I've only been gone half a year!' Monkey laughed, sweeping back onto his throne.

'Remember that one day in Heaven is a year on earth,' his generals reminded him. 'You've been gone well over a century. What job did the Jade Emperor give you this time?'

'This time,' Monkey reported, 'the Jade Emperor saw sense and appointed me Great Sage Equal to Heaven. He built me a palace and gave me two departments and a ministerial staff. But it turned out that I had nothing to do, so they put me in charge of the Orchard of Immortal Peaches. When the Queen Mother failed to invite me to a banquet, I crashed her palace and secretly guzzled all the food and wine for the feast. Then I stumbled by mistake into Laozi's palace, and since he wasn't around I polished off all his elixirs. After that, I decided to lie low for a while. So here I am.'

Elated by this update, Monkey's monstrous audience assembled fruits and wine for a welcome-home banquet. After filling a stone bowl with coconut wine, they proffered it respectfully to Monkey. The Great Sage took a gulp and grimaced. 'That is disgusting!'

'Coconut wine, it's true, bears no comparison to the food and wine of the immortals,' replied two of his generals. 'But as they say: east, west, home's best. This is the local brew.'

'I spotted many more jars of that scrumptious wine at the Queen Mother's place this morning,' said Monkey. 'Give me a moment and I'll filch another few bottles. After half a cup, you'll all become immortals.' While the monkeys practically effervesced with anticipation, the Great Sage bounced out of the cave and again under cover of invisibility somersaulted back to the Festival of Immortal Peaches, where he found the winemakers still snoring soundly. Tucking two large bottles under each armpit and taking another few in each hand, he spun his cloud around and returned to Water-Curtain Cave, where thanks to the wine of immortality, a thoroughly good time was had by all.

Back to the ladies-in-waiting now. When Monkey's immobilizing magic finally wore off, after a whole day, they went straight to the Queen Mother to explain why they were so late. 'How many peaches did you manage to pick?' the Queen Mother asked.

'Only two baskets of small peaches and three baskets of middle-sized peaches,' her ladies replied. 'When we looked in the back of the orchard, there was just one big peach. We suspect that the Great Sage has eaten them all. While we were looking for peaches, he suddenly popped up out of nowhere and threatened to beat us. He also wanted to know who had been invited to the banquet. When we didn't mention his name, he immobilized us all. We've no idea where he went next.'

The Queen Mother immediately went to inform the Jade Emperor. But before she could complete her report, the crowd of winemakers turned up to file their own complaint. 'An unidentified individual has sabotaged the Festival of Immortal Peaches by drinking the jade wine and eating the hundred delicacies.'

Finally, in marched Laozi, who got quickly to the point: 'Person or persons unknown have stolen the top-quality elixir I was smelting for your Majesty's personal use.'

While the Jade Emperor reeled at this catalog of theft, the departmental aides from Monkey's mansion turned up. 'The Great Sage hasn't been seen since yesterday. We've no idea where he is.'

Just as the emperor was putting two and two together, the Barefoot Immortal prostrated himself before the throne. 'I ran into the Great Sage Equal to Heaven yesterday while on my way to the Queen Mother's festival. He told me that the Jade Emperor had ordered all the guests to attend a rehearsal in the Hall of Perfect Brightness, but no one was there when I turned up.'

The Jade Emperor's astonishment grew further. 'This fellow falsifies my decrees and deceives my ministers. Tell the Spirit of Public Security to get to the bottom of this.'

The divine detective immediately began his investigation and soon returned with a thick dossier of evidence. 'The criminal responsible for wreaking havoc,' he concluded, 'is none other than the Great Sage Equal to Heaven.' Outraged, the Jade Emperor ordered his Four Great Heavenly Kings to assist Heavenly King Li and Prince Nezha in bringing Monkey to heel. Together, they mobilized the Twenty-Eight Constellations, the Nine Luminaries, the Twelve Heavenly Branches, the Guards of the Five Quarters, most of the Heavenly officer corps, plus one hundred thousand celestial infantry. Dust and fog billowing about them, this vast expeditionary force descended to earth, encircling Flower-Fruit Mountain so tightly that not even a drop of water could slip through, and spread eighteen cosmic nets to make aerial escape impossible. The Nine Luminaries led their troops in a vanguard attack on the entrance to the cave, where they discovered an enormous throng of monkeys of all sizes prancing about and generally having a fine time.

Monkey King Makes Havoc in Heaven

'Puny demons!' roared one of the spirits. 'Where is your leader? We are gods dispatched to subdue the rebellious monkey. Tell him to surrender immediately. The merest whisper of resistance and we'll turn the lot of you into baboon butter.'

The panicked monkeys rushed into the cave to report the uninvited guests: 'Calamity, Great Sage! Nine fierce gods are outside saying they've come to subdue you.'

Just then, Monkey was enjoying a few cups of heavenly wine with seventy-six of his closest friends. He seemed perfectly unfazed by the news of what was going on outside. 'Drink your wine while it's warm,' he proverbialized. 'Never mind the brewing storm.'

Another cohort of fiends charged over. 'Those rough gods say they're about to break down the door.'

'Seek not worldly fame or gain,' the Great Sage continued. 'Except wine and verse, all is in vain.'

Now a third gaggle of monkeys barreled up. 'They've smashed in the door and are fighting their way into the cave.'

At this, Monkey lost his temper. 'How rude! And after I'd treated them so nicely!' He ordered the Rhinoceros-Horned Monster Kings to lead the other monstrous monarchs into battle, while he and his generals brought up the rear.

After the vanguard was quickly bogged down in an ambush set by the Nine Luminaries at the mouth of the iron bridge, Monkey extended his staff to twenty feet and threw himself into the fight. 'Make way for Monkey!'

The Nine Luminaries were instantly beaten into retreat. 'You stole the immortal peaches and the immortal wine, you wrecked the Peach Festival, then swiped Laozi's immortal elixirs and plundered the divine brewery a second time,' they shouted at him after regrouping. 'What do you have to say for yourself?'

'Stuff happens!' Monkey laughed back. 'What of it?'

'The Jade Emperor has ordered your capture. Surrender now, and your people will live. If not, we will raze this mountain to the ground.'

The threat enraged Monkey out of his nonchalance. 'Enough of your hot air, you pesky gods – meet my staff!'

Even with the Nine Luminaries leaping simultaneously at him, Monkey easily fought them to exhaustion. One by one, they fled the battlefield and returned to camp, dragging their weapons behind them. 'He's got guts, this monkey,' they admitted to King Li, who now dispatched the Four Heavenly

Kings and the Twenty-Eight Constellations into battle. Monkey serenely arranged the monstrous monarchs and four generals in formation outside the cave, where battle resumed at dawn. After a day of epic, murderous combat, the Heavenly army had taken all the monstrous monarchs captive; only the four generals and the monkey minions managed to escape back inside the cave. Monkey, meanwhile, single-handedly held the Four Heavenly Kings, King Li, and Prince Nezha at bay in a duel in midair. As dusk fell, he pulled out a handful of hairs, chewed them up, and changed them into thousands of specious Monkeys, each with their own golden-hooped staff; together, they beat the Heavenly commanders into retreat.

The victorious Monkey retrieved his hairs, rushed back into the cave, and delivered a philosophical speech to his troops, whose morale had been battered by the capture of the monstrous monarchs. 'Victory and defeat are the lot of all armies. To kill ten thousand enemies, you may have to sacrifice three thousand of your own. On the bright side, our losses were all tigers, leopards, wolves, snakes, and badgers. We monkeys are safe and sound. Stay strong! My body division magic has temporarily beaten our enemies back, but they are still camped at the bottom of our mountain. We must eat, sleep, and be vigilant. When morning comes, I will avenge our comrades by capturing Heaven's generals with a fantastic magic trick.' And after a few bowls of coconut wine, all the monkeys fell asleep.

Chapter Six

Before things had started to go so wrong in Heaven, the Queen Mother had invited the great compassionate Bodhisattva Guanyin from Mount Potalaka in the South Sea to the Peach Festival. But when Guanyin, with her senior disciple, Hui'an, arrived at the Jade Pool, they found everything in disarray. After a handful of busily gossiping immortals had given her a sketchy account of what had happened, she went straight off to see the Jade Emperor, who was seated on his dais next to Laozi, with the Queen Mother behind the throne.

'So what's this business about the Peach Festival?' Guanyin asked, after exchanging greetings with the three of them.

'Usually it's the highlight of the social calendar,' complained the Jade Emperor, 'but this year that demonic monkey has spoiled the whole thing. We've had to cancel all the invitations.'

'And where did this demonic monkey spring from?' Guanyin next wanted to know.

The Jade Emperor explained Monkey's backstory: his emergence from a stone egg on top of Flower-Fruit Mountain, his radiating shafts of golden light as far as the Palace of the Polestar, and so on. 'We didn't think anything of it at the time, but then he went on to make a real pest of himself, bullying dragons, getting himself and his minions deleted from the registers of life and death. My first thought was to take him captive, but the Spirit of Longevity thought he might have potential as an immortal. Hoping to civilize this magic monkey, we therefore summoned him to Heaven and put him in charge of the imperial stables. After he absconded, claiming the job was unworthy of him, we offered him an amnesty and an honorary title, Great Sage Equal to Heaven. To keep him out of trouble, we put him in charge of the Orchard of Immortal Peaches. But he ate all the biggest peaches (without permission, I might add), smuggled himself into the peach banquet (to which he had *not* been invited) disguised as Barefoot here, polished off all the food and wine, stole Laozi's elixirs, and thieved some more wine to share with his goblins down below. Since we are not amused, we have dispatched one hundred thousand soldiers with cosmic nets to bring him to heel. We're still awaiting news from the battlefield.'

Guanyin now told Hui'an – who also happened to

be the second son of King Li, the heavenly general – to go to Flower-Fruit Mountain. 'Help out on the battlefield, if they need it. Then come back and tell us exactly what's going on.'

Approaching by cloud as dawn broke, Hui'an found the mountain thickly shrouded in overlapping nets, guarded by sentries shouting passwords at one another. 'It's Hui'an, second prince of King Li, Guanyin's senior disciple,' he told them. 'I've been sent to inquire about the state of play here.' Once the message had been passed on to the king, the sentries were ordered to open the net and admit Hui'an, who immediately went to kowtow before his father and the other commanders.

'What are you doing here, my boy?' asked King Li.

Hui'an explained his mission: 'Since no one in Heaven had heard anything about the campaign for a while, the Bodhisattva dispatched your stupid, unworthy son to bring news.' King Li recounted the events of the previous day and explained that although they had captured some wolves, snakes, tigers, leopards, and badgers, all the monkeys were still at large.

At this moment, a sentry appeared. 'The Great Sage is outside the camp with an army of feral monkeys, all baying for a fight.'

The heavenly kings immediately set to discussing

battle formations. 'Guanyin said I should lend a hand, if necessary,' Hui'an interrupted. 'Why don't I go and size up this Great Sage?'

King Li accepted his offer. 'I'm sure you've learned a lot from Guanyin. But do be careful.'

Cinching his embroidered robe and grasping an iron staff, Hui'an leaped out of the camp. 'Where is this Great Sage Equal to Heaven?' he hollered.

'None other,' replied Monkey, raising his own staff. 'Who dares ask?'

'I am Hui'an, the second son of King Li, senior disciple of the Bodhisattva Guanyin of the South Sea.'

'What are you doing here?'

'Guanyin sent me to find out what was going on. Given what a nuisance you've been, I've decided to arrest you.'

'Big talk from a little squirt,' responded the Great Sage. 'But don't leave just yet. I want to introduce you to this staff of mine.'

The two of them fought like whirlwinds until eventually Hui'an's arms and shoulders began to ache. With one last weak swing of his staff, he fled back inside the camp to report his defeat. 'That monkey is extraordinary!' he panted. Shaken by this latest setback, King Li dashed off a request to the Jade Emperor for reinforcements and sent Hui'an and another king back up to Heaven to deliver the message. An instant later, the two of them were in front of Guanyin and the Jade Emperor, who tore open the note asking for backup.

'Ha!' the emperor snorted. 'Can this monkey really be powerful enough to defeat one hundred thousand celestial soldiers? Who else can we send?'

'How about your nephew, Erlang, from the River Guan?' Guanyin suggested. 'The one who killed six monsters and whose followers include the Brothers of Plum Mountain and twelve hundred plant-headed spirits. These days, he only takes on special missions.'

Dashing off another order, the Jade Emperor sent it to Erlang by express cloud. The envoy recapped the state of play with Monkey and the Jade Emperor's request for Erlang's assistance: 'Success will result in promotions and rewards all around.'

Erlang instantly accepted the challenge and summoned his followers. After a quick mission briefing, they harnessed hawks and dogs, primed bows, and set out across the Eastern Ocean on a particularly violent gale. In the twinkling of an eye, all landed on Flower-Fruit Mountain and were let into the cosmic nets. 'I'm ready for this monkey,' Erlang said, smiling at the expedition's commanders. 'If he gets the better of me, my blood brothers will lend a hand. Just make sure that the cosmic nets are left open at the top. King Li, please stand by in midair holding a demon-reflecting mirror. Should he be defeated, I fear that he will try to flee – the mirror will reveal his whereabouts.'

Erlang now led his people out of the camp: his blood brothers from Plum Mountain were to goad Monkey into a fight, while the plant-headed spirits were to hold the defensive line and ready the dogs and hawks for battle. At the entrance to Water-Curtain Cave, Erlang found a tidy column of monkeys beneath a banner that read THE GREAT SAGE EQUAL TO HEAVEN. 'The nerve of the creature!' spluttered Erlang.

'Save your outrage for later,' urged his brothers. 'Just challenge him!'

Meanwhile, a monkey sentry had reported Erlang's arrival to the monkey king, who pulled on his best armor and charged out of the cave to size up his new adversary. Erlang cut a remarkable figure: exquisite features, bright eyes, shoulder-grazing earlobes. He wore a robe of pale yellow goose down, with a jade belt and gold boots. A crescent bow hung from his waist; his hands played with a tri-pointed lance.

'Where did you come from, shrimp?' Monkey taunted, spinning his staff.

'What a question!' roared Erlang. 'I am Erlang, maternal nephew of the Jade Emperor, King of

Extremely Obvious Brilliance by Imperial Appointment. I'm here on His Majesty's orders, you mutinous macaque, to bring you to justice. Lost the will to live yet?'

'I do have a vague memory,' Monkey mused, 'of the Jade Emperor's marriage to a mortal by the name of Yang. I presume you're their undersized offspring. One touch of my staff will turn you into pip-squeak pâté, but I bear you no grudge and I'd like to spare your life. Off you trot now. Tell your Four Heavenly Kings to come instead.'

Erlang responded to the invitation by aiming at Monkey's head and bringing his lance down hard. Dodging the blow, Monkey returned the compliment with his own staff. This murderously close duel raged through three hundred clashes; deputies on both sides waved banners and beat drums. With no clear winner emerging, Erlang decided to mobilize some magic, suddenly towering a hundred thousand feet tall. Monkey instantly replicated the trick. Noticing that the monkey generals were distracted by this display, Erlang's blood brothers ordered the plant-headed spirits to release hawks, hounds, and arrows at the entrance of Water-Curtain Cave. Caught off guard, several thousand little monkeys were captured while the rest scattered, shrieking, like a nest of dozing birds startled by a cat.

Knocked off balance by the flight of his followers, Monkey shrank back to his real size, pursued by Erlang. Trying to flee into the cave, he was blocked by Erlang's six blood brothers. Panicking, Monkey pinched his staff to the size of an embroidery needle, tucked it inside his ear, changed into a sparrow, and perched on a treetop. 'Where did he go?' exclaimed the discombobulated brothers.

Keeping a cool head, Erlang saw through Monkey's transformation with his magic third eye. Discarding his weapons, Erlang turned into a falcon and rushed at the sparrow, which soared upward, now as a cormorant. Erlang smartly became a large sea crane, drilling into the clouds with its bill. The Great Sage changed direction, plunging into a stream as a fish. Erlang – now a fish hawk – skimmed over the surface of the water. Monkey swam off in the opposite direction, leaving a trail of bubbles. 'There's something odd about that fish,' mused Erlang. 'It has the look of a carp but no red tail. There's something of the bream about it, but it has no gill bristles. And why did it make off as soon as it saw me? I smell Monkey!' Just as Erlang's beak dipped into the water, Monkey flung himself onto the bank as a water snake and slithered off into the grass. Erlang turned into a vermilion-headed gray crane and pounced with his pincerlike beak at the fake snake, which promptly became a spotted bustard, perched stupidly amid the knotweed. Seeing that Monkey had transformed strategically into such a degraded creature – the spotted bustard is the lowest and most promiscuous of birds, mating carelessly with phoenixes, hawks, and crows – Erlang refused to go anywhere near him. Returning to his true form, he shot the bustard with his pellet bow, sending the bird hurtling off balance.

After rolling down the mountain a way, Monkey laid low for a while, then transformed into a small temple to the local spirit: his mouth became the entrance, his teeth the doors, his tongue the statue of the Bodhisattva, his eyes the windows. His tail proved a puzzler, though, until he eventually decided to stick it up in the air as a flagpole. The approaching Erlang sized up the shrine with that useful third eye of his. 'That monkey's trying to fool me again. I've seen plenty of temples in my time, but never one with a flagpole. If I go in, he'll gobble me up. I'd better smash the windows and kick the door in.' Anticipating that this would hurt, Monkey sprang into the air and disappeared again.

As Erlang looked around him, his six blood brothers caught up; after briefing them quickly, Erlang told the others to keep a lookout while he went to check on King Li and his demon-reflecting mirror on the cloud tops. 'Have you seen that Monkey?' Erlang hollered.

King Li shone his mirror in all directions. 'I see him!' He laughed. 'He's made himself invisible and is on his way to your own stomping ground, the River Guan.' Erlang hurried off in pursuit.

As soon as he reached the Guan, Monkey changed himself into an exact likeness of Erlang, received the obeisances of Erlang's subordinates, and set to officiating in his nemesis's own temple. Not long after, however, the real Erlang arrived, and his officials rushed out to see the doppelgänger. 'Has a so-named Great Sage Equal to Heaven been here?' Erlang wanted to know.

'No, no one of that name. But there is another version of you inside.'

After the real Erlang charged at his impersonator, Monkey took his true form. 'Welcome to the Temple of Monkey!' Erlang struck at Monkey's face with his tri-pointed lance, but Monkey dodged, and the two of them jousted their way back to Flower-Fruit Mountain.

Back in Heaven, the Jade Emperor and his court were wondering why they had heard no news of Monkey for some while. Guanyin suggested they go out to see for themselves. 'Good idea,' agreed the Jade Emperor, and sent for his carriage. From the South Gate, they could see Erlang battling Monkey within the cosmic nets, with King Li and Nezha floating on top, holding the demon-reflecting mirror.

'Erlang has Monkey surrounded, if not quite in the bag,' concluded Guanyin. 'Time for me to give him a hand.'

'How?' Laozi asked.

'I'll throw my willow vase at him. It will stun him long enough for Erlang to apprehend him.'

Laozi was doubtful. 'If he gets his iron staff to it, he'll smash it to bits. I've a better idea.' Rolling up his sleeve, he shook a bracelet off his left wrist. 'This steel circlet is infused with ingenious magic, impervious to fire and water, and can trap all manner of creatures.'

Dropped from Heaven, the snare hit Monkey squarely on the head as the battle with Erlang and his brothers was reaching a fever pitch. Losing his balance, Monkey stumbled and fell. As he tried to pick himself up, one of Erlang's small dogs bit him on the calf. 'Get lost and chomp on your master!' Monkey cursed. Before he knew it, Erlang and his brothers had pinned him down, trussed him with ropes, and punctured his shoulder blade to prevent him from transforming again.

Laozi retrieved his circlet and suggested that the

Jade Emperor and his retinue return to the Hall of Divine Mists, while the expeditionary forces congratulated themselves on a job well done and packed up for home. In no time at all, the triumphant commanders returned to Heaven, caroling songs of victory. Erlang was richly rewarded – with a hundred golden flowers, bottles of wine, tablets of elixir, and countless other treasures – and sent back home. The felon, the Jade Emperor decreed, was to be taken to the Demon Execution Block and chopped into small pieces, to put an end, once and for all, to Monkey's grandiloquent tricks.

Chapter Seven

The Heavenly executioners tied Monkey to the Demon-Defeating Pillar on top of the Demon Execution Block. There, they chopped him with a knife, minced him with a hatchet, stabbed him with a spear, and slashed him with a sword – all without the slightest effect. The Star Spirit of the South Pole ordered the Immortal Fire Department to roast him with fire, but that cut no ice, either; then he had the Immortal Thunder Department strike him with thunderbolts; again, Monkey was not bothered. 'This Monkey is unfathomably powerful,' the executioners reported back to the Jade Emperor. 'We've tried everything, but he's still alive.'

'What are we to do?' asked the Jade Emperor.

'This monkey,' Laozi explained, 'ate the peaches and drank the wine of immortality, and swallowed five calabashes of elixir. I expect that the contents of his stomach have been smelted into a magical mass that, united with his constitution, has made him almost indestructible. Let me slow-cook him in the Brazier of Eight Trigrams to extract the elixir; once that's done, he'll crumble to ashes.' The Jade Emperor told his security forces to hand Monkey over to Laozi, who took him directly to Tushita Palace. There, Laozi untied Monkey, pulled the knife out from his shoulder blade, and pushed him into the brazier, telling his attendant to stoke up a strong blaze. Smoke billowed inside the brazier, leaving Monkey's eyes permanently red and inflamed.

Forty-nine days rushed by, and Laozi's braising was complete. As soon as Monkey heard the oven door open, he sprang out, rubbing his eyes, kicked the brazier over, and charged out of the potions chamber. Laozi's attendants and the Security Department escort rushed to restrain Monkey, but – febrile after his confinement – he was too much for all of them. Laozi himself tried to apprehend Monkey but was shoved aside while Monkey made his escape. Taking his magic staff out of his ear, Monkey turned it into a cudgel and went on such a rampage that the Nine Luminaries and Four Heavenly Kings preferred to stay at home and pretend they couldn't hear anything. The slow-cooking, it seems, had only further refined Monkey's powers. With discipline, he might become a force for supernatural good; without it, he was pure animal – a wrecking ball in Heaven.

All this hullabaloo soon came to the attention of

the Jade Emperor, who promptly sent a pair of his ministers west to ask the Buddha to vanquish this problem monkey. The two made straight for Thunderclap Monastery on Soul Mountain, where – after the usual exchange of courtesies – they were ushered in to see the Buddha, and their whole sorry tale tumbled out. 'You're our only hope,' they pleaded.

'Look after the monastery,' the Buddha told his Bodhisattvas, 'and make sure no one slacks off their yoga. I've got a demon to exorcise.' He and his two senior disciples then traveled directly to the Jade Emperor's palace, outside which they discovered the untamable Monkey noisily encircled by thirty-six thunder gods. 'Put down your weapons,' the Buddha ordered the thunder gods, 'and tell the Great Sage to come and talk to me.'

After receiving the message, Monkey walked cantankerously over to the Buddha. 'Who are you? Can't you see I'm in the middle of a battle?'

The Buddha laughed. 'I am the venerable Gautama Buddha from the Land of Ultimate Bliss in the West. I have just learned of your rebellion against Heaven. Where were you born? When did you learn the Way? Why are you making such a nuisance of yourself?'

For reasons best known to himself, Monkey chose to answer in free verse:

Wu Cheng'en

Born of heaven and earth, infused with immortal
  magic,
I am a monkey from Flower-Fruit Mountain.
After making my home in Water-Curtain Cave,
I sought instruction in the mysteries of eternal life
And mastered the art of infinite transformations.
Since earth was too small for me,
I set my heart on the Jade Heaven.
No one can reign forever in the Hall of Divine Mists,
Just as king succeeds king in the human world.
True heroes dare to fight and win.
Strength is honor; and none are stronger than
  I. Yield to Monkey!

The Buddha was unimpressed by this performance. 'You're just a magic monkey,' he snorted. 'How dare you presume to usurp the throne of the Jade Emperor? He has been cultivating himself since he was a boy, 1,750 eons ago. An eon lasts 129,600 years. Do the math – that's how long it takes to master the Infinite Way. You, on the other hand, are merely an animal with pretensions to humanity. How dare you boast and curse like this? Repent, before you throw your life and talents away.'

'I don't care how old he is,' Monkey retorted. 'He should give someone else a turn as emperor. Me, for example. Tell him to get lost and give me his palace, and that'll be an end to it. If not, I'll make a rumpus he'll never forget.'

The Buddha tried a different tack. 'So you're immortal and fluent in the art of infinite transformation. What other skills can you bring to the role of emperor?'

'I can travel 108,000 miles in one cloud-somersault. Why, I'm grossly overqualified for the job!'

'Very well,' said the Buddha, 'I'll make a bet with you. If you can somersault out of the palm of my right hand, then you win. I'll tell the Jade Emperor to move in with me and turn Heaven over to you. But if you can't, then you'll go back to being a monster in the world below. It'll take you centuries to get anywhere near Heaven again.'

Monkey laughed to himself. *This Buddha's an idiot. His palm's less than a foot wide. How could I fail?* 'You swear?' he asked out loud.

'I swear,' confirmed the Buddha, opening his palm out like a lotus leaf.

'Back in a jiffy!' Monkey shouted, leaving behind only a vapor trail. All the while, the Buddha kept his Eye of Wisdom on him, watching as Monkey whirled forward like a pinwheel until he suddenly encountered five flesh-pink pillars surrounded by green air. *Looks like this is the end of the road. Hello, Hall of Divine Mists, good-bye, Jade Emperor.* The Buddha *promised!* Then Monkey had a second thought: *I should leave my mark, in case the Buddha tries to be slippery about it.* Pulling out a hair, he changed it – with a breath of magic air – into a thick writing brush soaked in ink and scrawled in large letters on the middle pillar: THE GREAT SAGE EQUAL TO HEAVEN WAS HERE. His inscription complete, he retrieved his hair and – I'm very sorry to say – deposited a stream of bubbling monkey pee at the base of the first pillar. With a reversal of his cloud-somersault, he was back to where he had started, standing on the Buddha's palm. 'Mission accomplished. Tell the Jade Emperor to pack up.'

'You never left my palm, urinous ape!' the Buddha roared.

'Don't be thick,' retorted Monkey. 'I went to the edge of Heaven, where I found five flesh-pink pillars surrounded by green air. I even left a little memento: come with me and I'll show you.'

'No need,' the Buddha responded. 'A glance down will suffice.'

Looking down, Monkey found – as promised – the words THE GREAT SAGE EQUAL TO HEAVEN WAS HERE written on the Buddha's middle digit and a reek of monkey piss at the fork of the index finger. 'What – what sorcery is this?' he gasped. 'I don't believe it! Let me have another go.'

But as our hero squatted for a second somersault,

the Buddha flicked Monkey out of the West Gate of Heaven and back to earth. The Buddha's five fingers became the five phases – metal, wood, water, fire, and earth – of Five-Phases Mountain, pinning Monkey beneath. 'Hurray!' the assembled deities clapped and cheered. Their monkey-extirpation job done, the Buddha and his disciples were about to leave when the Jade Emperor's chariot – canopied with jewels, drawn by eight bright phoenixes, escorted by wondrous music, and broadcasting blossoms and incense – drew up.

'You have saved us with your blessed presence!' the emperor effused to the Buddha. 'Please stay for the Great Banquet of Heavenly Peace so we can thank you properly.'

'Oh, it was nothing,' said the Buddha modestly. 'I am your humble servant. My powers pale in comparison to yours.'

The golden gates to the Jade Capitol, the Palace of Primal Mystery, and the Institute of Penetrating Light were thrown open, and the Buddha was invited to sit on the emperor's own dais. Some eleven thousand deities feasted on dragon livers, phoenix marrow, jade juice, and immortal peaches. There were divine dancing girls, there were zithers, there were gifts (including two pears and an auspicious purple fungus), and many, many toasts.

They were all blind drunk when an imperial inspector arrived to report that Monkey's head was sticking out from underneath the mountain. 'No matter,' said the Buddha. He fished out of his sleeve a plaque on which was inscribed in gold the Buddhist mantra OM MANI PADME HUM and told one of his disciples to fix it to a piece of rock on the top of the Five-Phases Mountain. The mountain immediately struck deep root, leaving just enough room for Monkey to breathe and move his paws about a bit.

The Buddha and his disciples now bid farewell to the Jade Emperor and his gods. Compassionate as ever, the Buddha, before returning to the west, appointed some protective spirits to guard the Five-Phases Mountain. When the prisoner was hungry, he explained, they should feed him iron pellets; when he was thirsty, he was to be given molten copper. When he had served his time, someone would release him, so that the baneful monkey could atone for his hubris by serving the Buddha. His liberator would be – one prediction went – a priest from the future Tang empire.

But as to when this person might come, the prophecy said nothing.

PENGUIN ARCHIVE

H. G. Wells *The Time Machine*
M. R. James *The Stalls of Barchester Cathedral*
Jane Austen *The History of England by a Partial, Prejudiced and Ignorant Historian*
Edgar Allan Poe *Hop-Frog*
Virginia Woolf *The New Dress*
Antoine de Saint-Exupéry *Night Flight*
Oscar Wilde *A Poet Can Survive Everything But a Misprint*
George Orwell *Can Socialists be Happy?*
Dorothy Parker *Horsie*
D. H. Lawrence *Odour of Chrysanthemums*
Homer *The Wrath of Achilles*
Emily Brontë *No Coward Soul Is Mine*
Romain Gary *Lady L.*
Charles Dickens *The Chimes*
Dante *Hell*
Georges Simenon *Stan the Killer*
F. Scott Fitzgerald *The Rich Boy*
Katherine Mansfield *A Dill Pickle*
Fyodor Dostoyevsky *The Dream of a Ridiculous Man*

Franz Kafka *A Hunger-Artist*
Leo Tolstoy *Family Happiness*
Karen Blixen *The Dreaming Child*
Federico García Lorca *Cicada!*
Vladimir Nabokov *Revenge*
Albert Camus *A Short Guide to Towns Without a Past*
Muriel Spark *The Driver's Seat*
Carson McCullers *Reflections in a Golden Eye*
Wu Cheng'en *Monkey King Makes Havoc in Heaven*
Friedrich Nietzsche *Ecce Homo*
Laurie Lee *A Moment of War*
Roald Dahl *Lamb to the Slaughter*
Frank O'Connor *The Genius*
James Baldwin *The Fire Next Time*
Hermann Hesse *Strange News from Another Planet*
Gertrude Stein *Paris France*
Seneca *Why I am a Stoic*
Snorri Sturluson *The Prose Edda*
Elizabeth Gaskell *Lois the Witch*
Sei Shōnagon *A Lady in Kyoto*
Yasunari Kawabata *Thousand Cranes*
Jack Kerouac *Tristessa*
Arthur Schnitzler *A Confirmed Bachelor*
Chester Himes *All God's Chillun Got Pride*

Bram Stoker *The Burial of the Rats*
Czesław Miłosz *Rescue*
Hans Christian Andersen *The Emperor's New Clothes*
Bohumil Hrabal *Closely Watched Trains*
Italo Calvino *Under the Jaguar Sun*
Stanislaw Lem *The Seventh Voyage*
Shirley Jackson *The Daemon Lover*
Stefan Zweig *Chess*
Kate Chopin *The Story of an Hour*
Allen Ginsberg *Sunflower Sutra*
Rabindranath Tagore *The Broken Nest*
Søren Kierkegaard *The Seducer's Diary*
Mary Shelley *Transformation*
Nikolai Leskov *Night Owls*
Willa Cather *A Lost Lady*
Emilia Pardo Bazán *The Lady Bandit*
W. B. Yeats *Sailing to Byzantium*
Margaret Cavendish *The Blazing World*
Lafcadio Hearn *Some Japanese Ghosts*
Sarah Orne Jewett *The Country of the Pointed Firs*
Vincent van Gogh *For Art and for Life*
Dylan Thomas *Do Not Go Gentle Into That Good Night*
Mikhail Bulgakov *A Dog's Heart*
Saadat Hasan Manto *The Price of Freedom*

Gérard de Nerval *October Nights*
Rumi *Where Everything is Music*
H. P. Lovecraft *The Shadow Out of Time*
Christina Rossetti *To Read and Dream*
Dambudzo Marechera *The House of Hunger*
Andy Warhol *Beauty*
Maurice Leblanc *The Escape of Arsène Lupin*
Eileen Chang *Jasmine Tea*
Irmgard Keun *After Midnight*
Walter Benjamin *Unpacking My Library*
Epictetus *Whatever is Rational is Tolerable*
Ota Pavel *How I Came to Know Fish*
César Aira *An Episode in the Life of a Landscape Painter*
Hafez *I am a Bird from Paradise*
Clarice Lispector *The Burned Sinner and the Harmonious Angels*
Maryse Condé *Tales from the Heart*
Audre Lorde *Coal*
Mary Gaitskill *Secretary*
Tove Ditlevsen *The Umbrella*
June Jordan *Passion*
Antonio Tabucchi *Requiem*
Alexander Lernet-Holenia *Baron Bagge*
Wang Xiaobo *The Maverick Pig*